DEGREES OF SEPARATION

Other Books by Ian Gouge

Novels and Novellas

On Parliament Hill - Coverstory books, 2021
A Pattern of Sorts - Coverstory books, 2020
The Opposite of Remembering - Coverstory books, 2020
At Maunston Quay - Coverstory books, 2019
An Infinity of Mirrors - Coverstory books, 2018 (2nd ed.)
The Big Frog Theory - Coverstory books, 2018 (2nd ed.)
Losing Moby Dick and Other Stories - Coverstory books, 2017

Short Stories

Degrees of Separation - Coverstory books, 2018
Secrets & Wisdom - Paperback, 2017

Poetry

Selected Poems: 1976-2022 - Coverstory books, 2022
The Homelessness of a Child - Coverstory books, 2021
The Myths of Native Trees - Coverstory books, 2020
First-time Visions of Earth from Space - Coverstory books, 2019
After the Rehearsals - Coverstory books, 2018
Punctuations from History - Coverstory books, 2018
Human Archaeology - Paperback, 2017
Collected Poems (1979-2016) - KDP, 2017

Non-Fiction

Shrapnel from a Writing Life - Coverstory books, 2022

Ian Gouge

Degrees of Separation

First published in paperback format, 2018
by Coverstory books; this edition 2022.

ISBN 978-1-9997840-6-5

Copyright © Ian Gouge 2018

www.coverstorybooks.com

for Hamish, Rebecca and Garsdale
- where this book started...

CONTENTS

The Waiting Room

(January 2017)

It was a cursory glance; the kind of sweeping, superficial look designed to absorb as much as possible in one movement, as if the most critical thing was to use one's eyes efficiently. He established the approximate size and scale of the room, its tone, an overall sense of feeling. The walls were part-panelled and painted a shade of brown that had been abandoned with a lost generation. Above the panelling they were an uninspiring cream punctuated with blocks of colour gifted from a number of large poster-sized displays. Inset the far wall, a painted wooden door of the same cream colour with no indication as to where it might lead; in front of him a tall free-standing wire rack - the kind that rotated unevenly with a squeak - was adorned with small postcard-sized leaflets.

The warmth surprised him. Outside the bitterness of the wind had whipped through his coat, and even the extra layer he'd debated needing had proven to be not entirely adequate. He missed the source of the heat in his initial sweep, not that he was looking for it. Automatically his hand pulled the woollen beanie from his head, loosed his scarf, and eased the zip on his fleece down a little, freeing his neck.

"Are you waiting for a train?"

Her voice startled him. In a sudden moment of recalibration, his eyes scanned again. She was standing facing one of the posters, her head turned his way. Slightly panicked, he checked to see what else he had missed, and only then saw the dark, pew-like bench down to his right and the rucksack that rested there, its predominance of orange somewhat at odds with the room overall.

She was a relatively small woman, with short curly hair mainly gone to grey. Her thick coat belied a frame which - from her size - was probably slight. In that instant he placed her anywhere between fifty and mid-sixties, and guessed she was probably more healthy than most of her peers: the walking boots, the rucksack, that slightly ruddy tone to her cheeks -

though that might just have been the extremes of heat and cold.

"No," he said, still slightly off-kilter with her sudden intrusion into his reality.

Although he had been to the States a number of times, he struggled to place her accent. American it clearly was, but it lacked the harshness or distinctiveness of the more obvious locations: New York, California, the deep South. It struck him - for no obvious reason - as something of a hybrid, a mongrel of an accent that might be the result of a partially nomadic existence, within the US if not further afield. He glanced at the rucksack again. It was well-travelled.

Having not returned her gaze to the display in front of her, he sensed an expectation that she wanted more from him. And why not? This was a deserted station with infrequent trains set in the middle of miles of winter moorland. Having a voice to interact with was potentially an exotic treat.

"I'm just out for a walk," he offered, trying to say enough to be accepted without giving anything of himself away. After all, why should he? "From a house down in the valley."

This seemed to be enough. She turned back towards the wall.

Forcing his hat into one of his fleece pockets, he made himself move, walking slowly towards the wire racking, adopting a pace that allowed him to overlay a second swath of detail on top of his initial impressions. The pace was important, not for him but for his companion. There was an unwritten convention about these things, about how you moved in an enclosed space when confined with just one other person - especially if that person were of the opposite sex and the location was remote. He needed to accepted as unthreatening - even though that was exactly what he was by nature. As he paused before the leaflets, he wondered if his current motion was how he naturally moved in public spaces like galleries and shops, and railway station waiting rooms: quietly, modestly, invisibly almost.

Timetables, conveniently placed at eye-level, were the first things he noticed; trains to and from the ends of the branch line that included this station. He picked one up and opened it. Most trains seemed to pass through, with only a few stopping each day. He checked his watch. If she were waiting for a train - as she surely must be - then she still had time to kill: either twenty or thirty-five minutes, depending on where she was heading. Instinctively he knew a time span of that magnitude made his presence there of greater value to her. He replaced the timetable and sifted through some flimsy brochures about local tourist sites. Given it was early January, he guessed most would be closed until Easter. If she was on holiday it could only be for the walking.

"This is interesting," she suddenly offered, turning to see where he now was in relation to her. "The history of the line here, and some of the disasters that happened in the early days. People died."

It was a further invitation, he knew that. He also knew his decision at this precise moment was a binary one. If he chose to ignore her, then doing so would be rude - and to an international visitor, too! Not that he felt any great loyalty to where he was; after all, he was something of a recent interloper himself. But he did have, of the two of them, the greatest claim to 'locality', to belonging there. Ignoring her would be problematic, effectively driving a wedge between them, compromising them both, and forcing him to cut short this temporary respite from the wind and drive him outside almost immediately. Re-encountering the cold so soon was not a prospect which appealed to him.

Only four steps were needed to locate him at her side. The exhibit showed three photographs that were fixed in time more by their sepia tones and fuzzy definition than the descriptive labels beneath them. In one, a small steam locomotive was off the rails, hanging perilously part way down an embankment. It seemed more motion freeze-frame than an image of its final resting place, though the text - as he read it - illuminated the event in explicit enough detail to confirm that it was indeed at such a jaunty angle that it came to rest.

"All those poor people," she offered.

Just beyond the locomotive's tender, the end of the first carriage could be seen pointing in a completely different direction and in such a way that the rest of the train could only be hanging further out of sight down and away from the tracks. The second coach - where all the deaths had occurred - was impossible to see. Perhaps it was better that way.

"Was it going too fast?" he asked, realising that getting her insight would be the fastest way to assimilate the story.

"The track broke," she said.

There was a short pause as he skim-read the poster, then glanced across to its companion piece on the same wall. Her voice brought him back.

"Would you like some coffee?" Seeing his instant confusion, she clarified. "I have a flask in my rucksack and a spare cup. For the cold."

*

"Where are you from?"

Having extracted the thermos and cups, she had placed the rucksack on the floor and they were now sitting side-by-side on the bench.

"Originally? A smallish place in Indiana. South Bend."

"Notre Dame?"

"Yes! How do you know that?"

"I used to travel to the states with work a few years ago," he explained. "Went to Chicago and then down to Warsaw, Columbus, Cleveland. I liked to drive rather than fly - at least while it was still a novel experience."

She smiled.

"My dad was in the military, so he tended to move a round quite a bit," she said. "At first just in the States, and then he was posted to England towards the back end of the war. Afterwards - once I was old enough - we had some time in Europe following him around before we went back home."

"Whereabouts?"

"In Europe?"

"No, in England."

"Norfolk, initially. Then down on the south coast for a while. He worked in intelligence; was one of the few Americans who could actually speak more than one language, so he was 'useful'." She smiled to herself.

"That must have been exciting, growing up seeing all those places?"

"I guess so, though I don't remember that much of it." She didn't sound convinced. "Maybe a bit like your experience of the US; the novelty wears off after a while."

Now that he was closer to her, could hear her speak, judge her from the gestures her body made, he guessed that she was probably in her early sixties - though she could easily have passed for a few years younger. If he were right, then she would have been born a few years after the war, which would have made her just an infant when trailing across Europe.

"After Germany, he was posted back to the UK for a few years, near Harrogate. So I went to school here for a while before we went back home."

He smiled to himself. So that explained the accent.

"So this is, what, a coming home of sorts?"

She laughed.

"Not exactly. I haven't been in the UK since - when? - maybe the early eighties. My dad died a while ago and I lost my husband in the middle of last year, so I decided that I'd take one last chance to revisit some those places from my childhood - places I really don't remember. Being separated from Jim and my dad made me realise that I was separated from my childhood somehow too. I thought it was right to try and fix that while I could."

"So that's why you're here."

"A mad American woman in the Pennines - she needs to have a reason, doesn't she?!"

They both laughed.

"I still have one or two acquaintances here. Kids I part grew up with. Of course they're older now too, and we haven't seen each other for years, so it's all a bit weird. But it's kind of cool too. And getting out to walk in the hills again is just brilliant."

"Even if it's a little cold?"

"Cold?" She was taking his empty cup from him. "Have you been to Chicago in the winter?"

He shook his head.

"I thought not."

He watched her as she put the flask and cups back into her rucksack then fastened the neck of the section that housed them. She stretched briefly then checked her watch. He sensed something of the effort in her stretch; it was the movement of someone who used to find such things much easier. He thought she was going to sit back down, but evidently she decided against it.

"What about you?" she asked, rocking gently up on her toes to work her calf muscles.

"Me?"

"I'm guessing that you're not from around here either - at least not in an everyday kind of way."

Even though it was a question he had asked himself - and specifically asked himself before he had booked the cottage just outside of Hawes - he knew that any made-up answer, however plausible, would be somehow inadequate. He rose too and took a few steps further into the waiting room.

"Not from here, no. Well, not in the sense of living here at any rate. I'm just renting for a week."

"A kind of holiday?"

"Kind of." 'Holiday' didn't seem the right word to use.

"A break, maybe," she suggested, sensing his difficulty and trying to help him out.

"That might be better." He paused for a second. "I know Yorkshire well enough; Yorkshire and Cumbria. I've had lots of holidays here over the years so I suppose the whole area has a special resonance for me. Familiarity, if nothing else."

"But why now?" She asked, checking her watch again. "Taking a break in freezing January?"

He looked up from his own watch. He sensed from her lack of urgency that she was catching the later of the two trains - so up to Carlisle, then. Had she not been doing so, surely she would have been hoisting her bag to her shoulder and making her way out onto the platform for the Leeds train that was perhaps just a minute or two away.

"What was the word you used? Separation? That resonates with me a little bit. Maybe, like you, I'm trying to get reconnected."

Her laugh surprised him.

"But you're not like me at all!" she said, her accent momentarily broadening. "You're still young; still have things to connect to afresh, surely. Things to look forward to."

The notion that he still possessed 'youth' made him smile. From his side it felt a little like a stupid grin, but he couldn't stop himself.

"I'm not sure about the young bit," he said, "but of course you're right about having things in front of me, ahead as it were. Both known and unknown."

"And doesn't that make life exciting?"

"The unknown?"

"Absolutely!"

From many other people that might have been interpreted as a trite 'typically American' shallow observation; a paper-thin sliver of truth stolen from the inside of a cheap Christmas cracker. Yet even after just twenty minutes or so, he knew she didn't mean it like that. She was a sincere and honest woman. He was surprised to find himself thinking that it would have been good to know her longer, to have been acquainted with her before.

"But what about your 'reconnections'?" she asked, bringing him back. "To what?"

"I don't know."

She raised her eyebrows in disbelief.

"OK. Well, maybe I do," he said hesitantly.

"And?"

"It's difficult to put into words really." He hesitated; it was. "And it sounds corny, trite. A bit pathetic actually."

"Try me, hon."

The casual appellation was not lost on him.

"Myself, really. I've been busy, you know. And there's been a lot of other 'stuff' going on. It takes all your time, I suppose. You get absorbed by it."

"You lose yourself a little bit, don't you?" she offered, sensing his struggle. He nodded. "I know what that feels like. Crappy isn't it? My dad was ill for ages before he passed. Without mom there, it all fell to me really; the looking after, the fixing things. I became an offshoot of him in a way, rather than my own person. I didn't see it until it was too late. Jim saw it. He warned me. But I was too stubborn."

She paused, then bent towards her bag. He had been wrong about her taking the later Carlisle train. Somewhere a bell sounded.

"I lost Jim before I lost my pop. And then I lost Jim again. And then I suppose I realised that somewhere along the way, I'd gotten lost too. Separated. Good word, isn't it?"

Suddenly she had shouldered her bag then took a step towards him, placing her hand on his arm.

"I need to git," she said, winking slyly. "You take care of yourself."

He leant forwards and kissed her cheek. It was a gesture as foreign to him as anything he could imagine, and yet it seemed perfect under the circumstances.

Her smile broadened. As she placed her hand on the door knob, she turned.

"Now you just be careful young man, or I might just be coming back here to see you again."

And with that she and her laugh were absorbed by the sudden arrival of the Leeds train which, just a minute or so later had whisked her invisibly away and out of the station.

He found himself alone. Now the waiting room was indeed how he had first perceived it: the panelling, the door, the wire rack, the outmoded cream walls, the emptiness. Glancing to the left of the exit, the long dark wooden bench was unladen. No flash of orange; no sign that there had ever been a rucksack there, a rucksack with a thermos of coffee and two cups inside.

Outside the wind had yet to relent. After the warmth of the waiting room, it bit into him remorselessly. Hoping it might make a difference, he pulled his beanie a little lower, and tugged his scarf up a shade. Out from the Carlisle-end of the platform he could see the spot where the engine had fallen, and in the mid-distance, just visible, the beginnings of the viaduct wall. Just five minutes ago another train had crossed there, rounded the corner safely, and come to rest at the platform.

Turning, he could see the tracks bending away towards the big hills that rose in the distance beyond, a feint trace of whiteness about their uppermost reaches. Yes, it was cold; but suddenly it was also good to be there in January.

He blew ineffectually on his gloves, then started back.

No-Man's-Land

(August 2008)

"I don't know," he said, a tone of frustration in his voice. "Do we always have to mean everything we say?"

"I hope so!" she replied, similarly upset. "Otherwise how do we know what's true?"

The heat didn't help. In addition to the persistent topic of Brigette's ailing father, a hot Indiana summer was just another thing to drive a wedge between them. Jim could manage well enough until the needle hit around ninety-five, but after that his temper shortened and he became increasingly brusque, even with Brigette. He recognised the failing and knew he shouldn't succumb to it, but his willpower, his self-control, was simply inadequate. Although he rarely showed as much publicly, this trait bothered him - and it especially bothered him now Brigette was struggling with her father. At least she had given up work, one of his suggestions she had acted upon. "After all," he had said then, "it's not as if we need the money." Having sewn the seed, it had taken her a few months to come round to his way of thinking, and once she had he'd seen an improvement in her very quickly - though she was clearly not yet quite back to her best.

But now they were arguing again. The return to some modicum of stability once freed from the burden of work had lasted perhaps two or three weeks at most. As they stood at either end of the kitchen, the table in the centre of the space something like no-man's-land, they found themselves combative again; quick to judge, to attribute motives, and all too ready to believe the worst. Jim knew this last part was a mutual failing. He expected it of himself because this was the person he had grown into, the one who had been shaped and nurtured by superficial and sometimes brutal parenting; but it was a new departure for Brigette, totally out of character.

He had forgotten precisely what the trigger had been this time. It didn't really matter. It was just sufficient to serve as a vehicle to escalate them into more nebulous and philosophical territory. Jim's weaknesses, once he had stepped into that particular threshold only served to agitate him further. Brigette always had the edge in such exchanges. Her jabs always landed, were cumulatively punishing. Backed onto the ropes, Jim resorted to the linguistic haymaker in the hope that one of them might land. Occasionally they did and usually with dreadful consequences. But such success (if you could call it that) seemed to occur less and less often these days - which only served to make him increasingly desperate.

Brigette's own desperation had little to do with winning or losing; from her perspective, as soon as the decibel level rose and irrationality crept in they were both losers. Her frustration related to loss of control - and on a number of levels too. She was always tired these days and her ability to manage anything - especially where Jim was concerned - was deserting her. These rows (which always seemed to manifest themselves in the kitchen or when they were together in the car) were evidence of that. She used to be able to steer, cajole, compromise; was emotionally intelligent enough for the both of them to ensure they navigated well through life. But it was that ability which had deserted her. She was fighting to keep control, but it was now more a fight in the gutter than the saloon and she was a poor brawler. What made it even worse was that scrapping levelled out the playing field somewhat, eroding any superiority she felt she had over Jim - a superiority needed in order to be able to keep them together as a single unit.

And that was what, underneath it all, scared her more than anything else. He was slipping away. And no matter how hard she tried, his drifting seemed unstoppable. It was a tide that showed no signs of turning. She guessed from his perspective contentious situations might look unlike anything she meant them to be; she knew he would most likely see her as an argumentative bitch, and now it seemed beyond her to appear any other way. The more desperate she got, the more she sensed that time was running out, the closer they edged toward a self-fulfilling prophecy.

This time it had been about money. Again. It was often about money these days. Supporting her father was an expensive business - both emotionally and financially. His insurance covered most of the costs, but she was committed, beholden almost, to try and make his life (what was left of it) as comfortable as she could. That meant indulging in what she liked to call 'little extras' but which she knew Jim saw as a waste of money. It wasn't really his fault. After all, given the kind of upbringing he'd had, how could he possibly understand an abiding love for - and warmth towards - one's parents, especially if it were one's only remaining parent? Jim was more likely to dig the grave *and* pull the trigger. She was conscious of arguing from a position of increased weakness given she was no longer earning any money of her own. These days when she spent, she was spending Jim's money. On at least one level, she knew he had a right to resent that, even just a little bit.

"Look, I didn't mean what I said…"

"Hang on," Jim interrupted, "a minute ago you were saying that we should mean everything we say!"

"No. OK. I did mean it, but not in the way you seem to have interpreted it." She tried to regather the threads that had loosened and were spilling out all around her. Perhaps if she could get a grip on them for long enough she might be able to tie them together, to braid them back into something useful. "I'll stop Jim, all right? If me trying to do the things I'm trying to do for Pop, the trying to make things a bit easier for him, if that's a problem because you don't think we can afford it…"

She let the sentence trail away, hoping for a sign, some clue from Jim that there was a compromise to be reached. Lately she'd been indulging her father more, that much was obvious. As he slipped further away from her, the measures she took to try and pull him back became increasingly extreme. Brigette had hoped that by bringing him into contact with replicas from his past, by buying him duplicates of the things he had once owned and treasured, she might be able to throw him a lifeline - one she could haul on from the other end. There were no indications that the strategy was in any way working; in fact, its only tangible outcome - other than the increasing volume of clutter which now seemed to surround him - was that for the third month in a row their bank account had seen more going out than coming in, and this time by a wide margin.

His features suddenly calming, Jim shook his head; the folded bank statement which had started this latest confrontation was still visible in the top pocket of his shirt. In spite of that it was a transformation that offered her no respite, no hope of conciliation or accord. He suddenly had a look of resignation upon his face - and the look of a man who had made a decision.

If that were the moment when the camel's back broke, Jim was not conscious of it; but something had suddenly wearied him beyond belief, and he knew, like a man drowning, that he needed to surface for air. It was probably callous in the extreme that he chose to ignore her plea and simply walked across the kitchen and out through the door behind her. It was a walk that seemed to possess purpose and yet from Jim's perspective was about nothing more than escape. He needed to be somewhere else.

She didn't try and stop him, didn't turn to watch him go, but rather gauged his progress by what she could hear: the door to the cupboard under the stair opening; Jim extracting something familiar; then the front door opening and closing. The sound of the Jeep starting up. "He's going fishing," she said to herself. And then, "That's good. That's what he needs. Some space."

When Brigette returned from visiting her father later in the day the Jeep wasn't in the drive, though she noticed fresh tyre tracks in the loose gravel. In their depth and sweep they seemed to betray agitation, anxiety. Although she was no expert in such matters, they looked like the kind of tracks one might leave if you were making a quick getaway.

Ostensibly nothing had changed inside the house. The strange air of foreboding she felt when she left to go to the hospice had lifted only marginally. From experience she knew such a worry was a thing of her own invention, merely a concern that something might have happened to her father since she had last seen him; that he might have slipped, declined somehow. That the self same nervousness remained on her return was sufficient to prove that it was caused by something else - and that the slipping away had nothing to do with her father.

Instinctively she went up to their bedroom first. At first glance there seemed nothing amiss, nothing shouted 'change' at her. And then she noticed things missing from Jim's side of the dresser: his after-shave, the spare set of office keys, his work phone. Opening the door to the large under-eaves cupboard at the top of the stairs, the space where the large red suitcase had been - the one they had bought to go to Florida all those years ago - screamed at her. Leaving the cupboard door open, she checked Jim's wardrobe and drawers. She guessed he had taken enough for perhaps a few days away; perhaps a week at most. Rather than an emotional reaction, she knew this represented calculation on his part and, as she sat on the edge of the bed, was something which only marginally took her aback. She wanted to be surprised, but failed. She wanted to be able to again say to herself "that's good; that's what he needs, some space" - but was unable to do so. She knew there was no point checking downstairs to see if he had returned his fishing rod to its normal home; it would still be in the Jeep.

That night she slept well. If she had expected some kind of collapse following Jim's departure, then she felt none. She busied herself making dinner after which, ignoring the single place she had set for herself at the kitchen table, she proceeded to eat sitting in front of an "It's a Wonderful Life" re-run on cable. Even faced with the ultimate pathos movie, she remained engaged but detached. It was a film that cracked Jim up so much he couldn't watch it any more; its affects on her were much more subtle.

Rising at her usual time the following morning, she took a long bath rather than a shower, mentally preparing herself for that morning's visit to see her father. Once out of the bath and dry, she examined herself closely in the bathroom mirror as she applied her usual minimal layer of make-up; little more than a dusting of foundation, the merest touch of mascara, no lipstick. She was surprised at the face which stared back at her. Not only did it show no outward signs of the previous day's trauma, if anything it seemed fractionally less careworn than in the recent past. If Denise from next door saw her when she made her way to her car, Brigette knew she might comment; Denise had an eye for such things.

It was rare that her father was awake when she arrived, and this day was no exception. He lay on his back, as usual, eyes closed, his face a picture of supreme relaxation. As she removed her coat and sat in the chair alongside his bed, she wondered - not for the first time - what might be going through his mind, what secret thoughts he might be thinking, how his life was behind those closed eyelids.

"No story today, Pops," she said, glancing at the small pile of Steinbeck on his bedside cabinet. He had always liked Steinbeck, and Brigette liked to read it to him as much for her own peace as anything else. It was another attempt at searching for a meaningful echo.

"Well, Jim's gone. I'm not surprised. Can't say I blame him really. And I guess you knew he would hightail it at some point, didn't you? You'd probably be too loyal to say that it was all my fault - but just let me know if that's what you think OK? I can take it." She paused to give him a chance to respond. There was nothing, of course. "Took some of his stuff - and his rods. I'm guessing that he'll be back to the house when he knows I'm not going to be there - he may be there now - and gradually take his other stuff, the things he needs. I'm pretty sure this is it, Pops. I don't think he's coming back. It's not temporary. I reckon he's been on the verge of doing this for a little while. And it hasn't mattered how hard I've tried. Didn't make any difference. Should I be surprised? I don't think so. In fact - and here's the weird thing - I'm kind of relieved." Another pause. "Really."

She took a sip from the Starbucks coffee she had collected at the 'drive thru' on the way over and reflected on what she'd just said.

"Is that a bit strange, Pops? Unnatural? Me being relieved at Jim's walking out on me? If you'd suggested it to me this time yesterday I would have told you that I'd be devastated, in pieces; that I'd wail and beg him to come back." She paused; more coffee. "You know what? I haven't even thought of calling him. Not once. Honest. Even though I guess that somewhere there's a part of me that still loves him. And why's that? Why haven't I called him? I thought about it before I came over. I had a long bath - for the first time in ages! - and played the whole thing out in my mind. And I was surprised. There was a part of me, a big selfish part that maybe I haven't been in touch with for a while, that was actually glad. Oh, I'm sure I won't be glad later, not when it sinks in, or when it gets to being 'practical'. But right now...? He's simplified things. Made it easier. On that basis, why should I want him back to make it even more complicated than it was before?! Now there's just the two of us. A third of my worry has just walked out the door, which just leaves me and you, doesn't it Pops? And it's not like you'll be going anywhere - no matter how much I might want that to happen. In a good way, I mean.

"And soon enough it will just be me; me and the world. Haven't had that experience for quite a while! Maybe I'll have to give it some thought. Maybe you can help me work out what I do next, when I'm on my own. 'Sure, that's fighting talk now,' I can hear you say, 'but what about later? It'll hit you later'. And you're probably right, like you always are. But I don't know, Pops. It might not be like that at all."

The Hero

(May 1964)

Built on the outskirts of Raleigh just a few years previously, their house turned out to be just about the right size - though for the wrong reasons. Before they had moved there had been debates about the number of rooms and the size of the yard, but these debates were never really from the perspective of the rooms or the yard themselves. Stella asked Harvey more than once whether they actually needed so much space, after all it was just the two of them at the moment. Not only was her relatively limp objection code for him to acknowledge the question of affordability, it was more pointedly a demand of Harvey to know what his intentions were in terms of a prospective family.

Stella was an only child. Apart from her uncle Hank way over in Washington State, all her family's units were pocket-sized; two children or more a rarity over singletons. As a clan, the Roscoes blamed Hank's five on his wife, a woman who - according to their preferred folklore - had become the epitome of profligacy in all its forms. They never said as much to Hank. They didn't dare. The big difference between Hank and the rest of them was that he could afford a big family; somehow he'd made money in the war. They said "he'd landed on his feet - even if it was in Seattle", and this seemed to give him carte blanche to divest himself of as many of the traditional Roscoe traits as he chose. Hank's path was not one Stella wished to travel.

But Harvey was made from a different mould. Neither successful nor rich like Hank, he was from a lineage whose tendency seemed to be to over-produce by default, even if they couldn't afford it. When the Roscoes and the Patissons got together gatherings were inevitably lop-sided, and not only in terms of the swarm of Patisson attendees. Where Stella's family were calm, mild-mannered, even timid on occasion, Harvey's tended towards the impulsive, expressive, hot-headed. Her parents assumed that, for Stella, this was a simple case of opposites attracting, and hoped - though it was a hope never articulated - that she would be able to calm Harvey down a little and that their offspring would benefit from a blend of the best of both.

Although she never said as much, this was Stella's hope too, even if her secret fear was that, once they were married, she would end up being swamped in exactly the same way the Roscoes as a whole were when the two troops got together. Therefore the house was a big issue for her. As far as she could see it was the most tangible statement of intent Harvey could make. Why did they need five bedrooms, unless he wanted four children? Why did they need such a large yard, unless it was to play touch football or practice baseball catching in? And where was the money going to come from even if he did have all these ambitions?

Harvey was a difficult man to stand up to, especially if you were Stella. He was kind and considerate, treated her well, spoiled her from time to time, was loving; so he was no threat from that perspective. But he needed to be right, needed to have his way. He was as solid and dependable a husband as perhaps she might have hoped for - but he was also a steamroller.

If would, of course, be fine. That's what he told her when she pressed him about money. He was doing well at work and there had been hints he would be up for promotion in the new year. So far 1952 had gone really well, the firm had beaten all the targets set, profits were on the rise. It might be a stretch in the short-term, but after a few months he expected to see his salary increase by about ten percent, "and that" he said with a flourish "will make us very comfortable!" Stella could never equate comfort with Harvey; he seemed a little to 'energetic' for that.

"Maybe we'll start with one, Honey, and see how we go from there." That had been his standard answer to the children question.

On the face of it, that suited Stella just fine. It was a sensible answer, and it implied that once they'd had one - and she *did* want to be a mother - there would be a suitable time for reflection, decision-making. She didn't know, for example, if she would be any good as a mother, even though the Roscoe genes seemed to produce natural maternal role models. Were she to follow that trend - and if she loved the process, the practicality of it - then why not? But if she were honest with herself, she really hoped to maintain the Roscoe tradition of small and compact. She also knew that in spite of the apparent consideration in Harvey's words, his outlook was most likely entirely different. He wanted a five-bedroom house because he wanted to fill it.

Before the end of 1952 Stella was pregnant.

Of course by May 1964 this was all ancient history, some of it forgotten, some passed into family folklore. Jim - the result of that pregnancy twelve years earlier - had heard about his great uncle Hank but mainly from the perspective of the remarkable collapse when his business failed and he discovered his wife having an affair with one of the managers in his office. Typically for Hank, the denouement had occurred swiftly and in a blaze of family publicity, culminating in him loading up the car one day and disappearing into the Rockies. A number of Roscoes had, in private at least, shaken their heads more than once and mused over what might have been had Hank stuck more closely to the tried-and-tested family mores.

Stella was a very different prospect in 1964 too, any remnants of the younger version of herself - the one who had agonised over the house, the size of family - now a distant memory for just about everyone, herself included. She'd had a hard pregnancy and by the time Jim arrived, painfully, in May 1953 she found herself keenly anticipating the conversation she and Harvey would soon be having with respect to the ceiling they were going to apply to the size of their family unit. Although she took to caring for Jim easily enough, by the time he was six months old, her experience of the previous twelve had set her own limit. And they had reached it.

Unfortunately, however - and much in the same way as the world had gone - Harvey was a changed man too. For the company in which he worked, the second half of 1952 was far from the glorious one they had anticipated, and as sales began to dwindle, so did the likelihood of his promotion. For a while he fought against it, trying to persuade himself that if he upped his game he might still be recognised as the stand-out guy. This ultimately wasted initiative saw him working longer hours for no more money, the only tangible consequence being that he was home less and less, and when he was there he was more and more tired. When this coincided with Stella's difficulties during her pregnancy - and subsequently the additional demands placed upon them both by the young Jim - he began to become more the kind of individual that her family had hoped he wasn't. Occasionally there were still bouts of kindness, displays of affection, but these became rare. A torpid monotony descended.

Even though Harvey's connection to his new son was fragile at best, his notion of family had not changed. Somewhere he still harboured the Patisson belief that a larger family was a better guarantee of happiness, and having been thwarted at work, he was determined to cling to that dream much like a man clinging to a life raft in an inclement sea. Because of his desperation, there was no conversation with Stella, no reasoned argument. They would have more children; no debate.

If there was a window during which Stella had the chance to escape, she didn't see it - or if she did see it, chose to ignore it. Her life was about to head exactly where she had not wanted and the only way out required the kind of bravery and self-belief she simply did not have. Two years after Jim was born she went through the same trauma for a second time - and once more two years after that. Even the arrival of Dawn, following on from Jim and Harvey Junior (known almost from the outset as 'Little H'), did nothing to assuage the awfulness of her situation. Neither did the arrival of a daughter soften Harvey as much as Stella had hoped. Gradually he emotionally distanced himself from all of them, and as the children started to grow and began to get a sense of how the world worked - including their timid mother and over-bearing father - they distanced themselves physically from him too. That last, unused bedroom, became a playroom; something of a sanctuary for the children.

In one of the corners of Harvey's study, a spare downstairs room that he occasionally used for reading and working but primarily for smoking and rumination, there was a large switch he had rescued from a tree felled a few years previously. It was about three feet long and tapered. It was Harvey's nuclear deterrent as far as his offspring were concerned; a weapon he had threatened to use on multiple occasions but never deployed.

That May, in 1964, for his eleventh birthday, Jim was rewarded with a new bicycle. All his friends had new bikes by this time and, having noticeably grown out of his old one, Stella had lobbied her husband on behalf of her son. It was, she had argued, almost two presents in one because it meant Jim could pass his current bike down to Harvey Junior; with a little servicing and perhaps a respray it would be as good as new. Whether Harvey was persuaded more by the emotional or the financial argument it was impossible to say, but Jim did get his new bike, his old one given over to Little H via a colleague of Harvey's who specialised in bike refurbishment.

Not far from their house was an old disused quarry. The site had been dug out for a short while during the war, but being fundamentally unproductive, had lain idle for the past eight or so years. There were rumours of the land around it being used for a brand new country club, the quarry being landscaped to form a centrepiece lake for the associated golf course. Thus far the rumours had proven to be no more than that, and when, on the 13th May, Jim took his new bike - and Little H with Jim's old bike - down to the quarry to play, it was part-filled as a result of recent spring downpours. Safe when it was dry, that day it was typically treacherous; the paths the boys used to cycle up and down were riddled with shallow puddles, especially so where water had run down the quarry side, gone across the path, and into the burgeoning lake below.

Coming to a narrow, twisting ledge, Little H had been cycling just in front of Jim when his back wheel started to slip. Although things happened very quickly, to Jim everything seemed to occur in slow motion. In any event he had enough time to recognise what was happening and that his little brother was in danger. With two or three rapid pumps of his own pedals, Jim managed to get close enough to be able to lean out from his bike and grab Little H just as his bike began to slide from beneath him. Seconds later the two boys were lying, wet and covered in mud, against the quarry wall, Little H somehow still holding on to his ride. Jim's friends who had witnessed the accident, told him he was a hero and that he'd saved his brother's life for sure. However, a hero was the last thing Jim felt when he realised that his actions had resulted in him sacrificing control of his own bike - his brand new bike - which now rested out of sight beneath the surface of the quarry's water.

Stella's subsequent entreaties on behalf of her son had little impact on Harvey. Even the testimony of Little H and all Jim's friends who had witnessed the event made no difference. Later the local newspaper would pick up on the story and come to take photographs of the two boys. Jim was publicly lauded. However, that day in the Patisson household Jim was taken into his father's study and the switch finally removed from its resting place.

For the remainder of his life, Jim consistently maintained that he had not cried when his father had beaten him. It was not an event he readily talked about though, and if pushed, would say that he remained steadfast because he did not wish his father to think he had won - and because he knew that he had done the right thing. To Little H, Jim was, of course, something of a Superhero; his own personal Captain America. And for Dawn, who would herself perpetuate the legend once she grew old enough to understand it, Jim took on the mantle of her protector - if only in her head, rather than in reality.

The household was fractured completely after that incident. All Harvey had succeeding in doing was to make even more tangible the wedge that had been growing between him and his family. Jim's beating allied Stella, Jim and Little H against him. Even at just eleven, Jim became the man of the family. They became a triumvirate united by shared loathing. Even

Dawn, lacking the experience to make up her own mind on the matter, was suitably swayed by the mood music within the house - and Little H's childish interpretation - to take the side of the majority.

For a while his local celebrity and his elevated standing in their household fuelled in Jim a sense of worth and righteousness that translated into a kind of superior tranquility. To his friends at school - those who had been party only to the newspaper gloss - Jim suddenly seemed older, more grown up. For a few this was just big-headedness arising from being 'in the news'.

In the end, the public approbation lasted perhaps a week or two - which was just as well, as Jim tired of the attention quickly. At home, however, the changes were more permanent. Having his mother and siblings unexpectedly lean on him, Jim was forced towards adulthood more quickly. Within a few months the age gap between himself and Little H in particular seemed to suddenly widen, and with it came a shift in Jim's attitude towards him. That he still loved his little brother was beyond question, but the fawning - either implied or explicit - became harder to take, and Jim began to spend less time with him. Within perhaps a year, their cycling together (never again down to the disused quarry) was a thing of the past.

Inevitably perhaps, this distancing was a sign of things to come. In many respects it was a microcosm of what was happening to all the relationships in the family: Jim with Little H, Little H with Dawn, Stella with herself, Harvey with everyone. They became a collection of individuals joined together by ever-loosening bonds. And no-one seemed bothered enough to want to re-tie the knots. With Jim's eventual departure for college and then his father's sudden death in the mid-seventies through a massive heart attack, the unravelling was complete.

If over the years the quarry bike story changed somewhat, that probably wasn't surprising. As Harvey Jnr. grew towards manhood, the notion of being beholden to his elder sibling rankled. Indeed, the dissatisfaction of being the minor partner in the story, the one who made the mistake, who was saved and therefore passive, began to grow from the moment he saw the focus and attention very clearly pointing towards someone who wasn't him. Yes, he was very much in the picture - how could he not be?! - but it felt a little like being the stooge to the *really* funny guy. Harvey Jnr. began to modify the story later: his brother having moved away, his father gone, his own adult journey now taking him north, there was nothing to stop a slight remoulding. By the time he had finished doing so, the outcome - two boys covered in mud, in peril from a near fatal accident in a quarry - was pretty much the same; however, what had changed was that Harvey Jnr. was no longer the cause. In his updated version they had come together whilst racing, both lost control, and somehow saved each other from sliding into the murky depths of the quarry. This retelling saw both bicycles lost and both boys getting the beating. And why not? After how his father had behaved, Harvey Jnr. had no real compunction in heaping more condemnation upon him.

A Small Cardboard Box

(November 1984)

"Come on in, Junior."

The speaker was smartly dressed, his suit and tie - grey and blue, and coordinated with the feint check in the suit cloth - spoke of his station and seniority. Although far from being a follower of fashion or a devotee of a 'chic' label, Brian knew that subtle touches made all the difference when it came to appearance. If the quality and 'look' of his working attire was just a cut above everyone else's, then that was by design. It demonstrated he was one of the top managers in the firm and that he had earned his relatively plush office. Unless he was suddenly upstaged - which he so rarely was these days - none of his staff were able to match him sartorially.

Strangely perhaps, Brian didn't regard his approach to his corporate persona as being competitive in any way. In his eyes it was a philosophy not based on a single ounce of one-upmanship, but rather driven by a need to look the part, of being able to demonstrate his fit to the role. It was about self-esteem. If he felt good and confident, that gave him a couple of points head start over just about everyone else.

Harvey Patisson was no exception. As physical specimens go, one might be excused for drawing parallels between the two men. Both were obviously on a downward trajectory from their heyday, though Brian had edged into his forties slightly more gracefully than the other and, if pushed, could still hold his own in a relatively competitive game of tennis. Brian was vaguely aware that Harvey - or 'Junior' as he liked to call him, having spotted his full name on his application forms four years previously - had been sporty in his youth. If you squinted your eyes as you stared back in time, it was just possible to see how he might once have looked. Now, sitting in the chair across from Brian's desk, the only image readily conjured was that of a man struggling to keep his head above water; a man in a tired suit.

The sobriquet 'Junior' had hung around for far too long, but it was only when his father died that Harvey could legitimately drop it. Any notion of him being 'junior' in the physical sense quickly disappeared too. Soon after he turned thirteen he underwent a growth spurt which saw him leapfrog both his mother and then his elder brother all within the space of about eighteen months. He tried to lose the suffix then, but given there was still a senior 'Harvey' in the family, he had little option but to metaphorically sit and suffer. His father's death just before he turned twenty proved a blessed relief - and not just from the perspective of his name.

Luckily his other nickname - 'Little H' - had been consigned to the dusty backroom of family mythology long before then. As soon as he passed five foot six or thereabouts and was starting to encroach on the eye-levels of the other two male members of his clan, everyone recognised that this particular childhood familiar now bordered on the insulting, and so they let it fade away.

In any event, the younger Harvey proved anything but little. His height grew in proportion to his overall mass, and even at fourteen he carried his 140 lb. frame lightly. You couldn't call him fat, partly because he wasn't, and partly because doing so would have potentially ignited the fiery temper he had inherited from his father. Harvey had been surprisingly lithe, quick too; there were murmurings of him trying out for the school football team at Linebacker, one if not two years ahead of the norm. Coach Davis thought he had 'it'. There were - for a while - rumours about a scholarship to some Ivy League establishment. His star-struck friends even whispered "NFL" from time to time. Harvey pretended not to listen, but the words stuck.

As it transpired, the name and temper were not the only things Harvey had inherited from his father. One might choose to be kind and call it 'bad luck' or karma, but the fact of the matter was that Harvey the younger also proved to be something of a failure. His father had - at least in his early days - been optimistic, prone to indulging a habit of fashioning impractical dreams and then trying to hold fast to them. But as time wore on and the dreams failed to materialise, usurped by the monotonous inconvenience of every day life, their evaporation changed who Harvey Senior was. The stars were similarly aligned for his second son.

Having had the possibility lodged in his head (admittedly by others at first), Harvey's stellar football career dissolved into nothingness like a mirage. There were a combination of factors: an ankle injury suffered when playing basketball, a slowing down of his upward growth, and a consequential problem in maintaining control over his weight - which unfortunately did not seem inclined to modify its pace in concert with his height. The college Linebacker trial failed to materialise as it became clear that these unexpected physical changes meant he could never be fit enough. The coach talked of 'power to weight ratios' as the 'it' got up and walked out. When this reality dawned on him, Harvey realised he had no back-up plan. At best, he was an average student; and the fact that he had pinned his hopes (consciously or not) on one day becoming an NFL millionaire, only succeeded in giving him permission to take his eye off the educational ball. Not only was he not going to get a scholarship for football, he might struggle to get one for anything else.

Timing was everything, of course. Even as he tried to knuckle down and make the best of a deteriorating situation, Jim was flying the family nest, away to college, away from North Carolina and up to Indiana. Harvey was left behind with his mother and younger sister. Although he tried as hard as he could, playing the role of the family's male domestic lead just didn't suit. If his mother saw too many echoes of his father in him, she refrained from saying so.

His current job suited him better than a number he'd previously had. It was not too taxing, not too repetitive, and he was not too bad at it. He liked the company well enough, and got along okay with his co-workers. Even his boss was a straight enough guy, and they had - more than once - found themselves the last men standing in a bar after a work's night out. Things had become a little rocky in the recent past, however. There had been a widely touted view that the LA Olympics would give the whole country a boost and that businesses which had been recently suffering - especially from overseas competition - would see a healthy rebound. Some businesses may have bounced, but Harvey's company was not one of them. And now Brian - his boss's boss - wanted to see him.

But then he wanted to see everyone. Surely that was a good thing? At least that's what Harvey and his cohorts had tried to convince themselves. People were scared of layoffs. Harvey had been there before, being given a small cardboard box and told to clear his desk. It was brutal and clinical. As he looked across at Brian, he had no way of telling where the conversation was going.

Of course other guys would have known, guys in sharper suits perhaps. Brian set out by giving a quick précis of the company's position. If he had a script, he didn't need to refer to it - after all, he'd already used it over ten times that day. The rumours were correct in the sense that business wasn't great; they weren't however accurate in terms of the depths of the problems they were facing. Harvey heard phrases like 'structural weakness' and tried to translate them into something he could understand. From way back came the notion of an offensive line with a sub-standard guard. That would be a structural weakness. It might mean the QB was vulnerable. If you had a flaw like that he knew it would have to be addressed.

"Which brings us to your department, Harvey." The switch from nickname to proper name was ominous. "Once we've made the changes we need to in Sales and Marketing - and we're making those changes today - we just won't need such a big team where you are. We don't want to, but we're going to have to let a few of you go."

Harvey suddenly noticed Brian was using 'we' all the time, simultaneously distancing himself from what was going on. Only a guy in a good suit and tie would know how to do that.

"I've already seen John and Rick, so they know."

"They're going?"

Brian nodded. "Good guys, both. It's a bummer, Harvey, but what can we do?"

Harvey liked Rick. Occasionally he was one of the last men standing too - though not today. He remembered the weekend they had driven over to Philadelphia to catch a Phillies' game. That had been a good weekend. They had been two behind in the ninth before the leadoff's homer and then the winning double right at the end when they were two and out.

"And I'm afraid," Brian's words brought Harvey back; back from the baseball game, back from Philadelphia, and back into Brian's office, "that brings us to you, Harvey…"

Don't Look Down

"Be early." That's what they had told him. "Be *really* early." Of course, he didn't know what 'really early' meant. He figured fifteen minutes would be plenty early enough.

They had chosen a small Italian restaurant around the corner from the hotel.

"Isn't that a bit 'low key'?" he had asked.

"The Old Man said that he doesn't want a fuss. He thought it would be, you know, nice for his last meal - sounds ominous! - his last 'official engagement' to be one-on-one with the guy who's taking over from him."

"Even if I'm young enough to be his son."

"You said that; he didn't."

And yes, Andy *had* said that - but he was pretty sure Brian had also thought it at some point. Wouldn't be human not to. He'd known 'The Old Man' for a few years now; not closely at first - why would they have been close? - but much more so in the recent past, especially when it became clear that he was one of a small number of people - maybe two or three - who had been identified as possible successors. Andy had assumed it wouldn't be him who was chosen, partly because he was the youngest, and partly because he wasn't American. But what did he know?! Enough not to need to be told that he had to be early.

He checked his watch as he turned the corner. About a hundred yards ahead, Brian was standing outside the restaurant looking his way. He raised his hand to acknowledge the younger man.

"Shit", Andy said to himself. Fifteen minutes had been nowhere near early enough. It was too late to matter now.

Being June, it will still light enough for Andy to get a reasonable impression of how Brian had chosen to dress for their dinner. Sartorially, he was one of the smartest guys Andy had ever met; it was a matter of pride as much as anything else. Brian knew he had a reputation for being a sharp dresser; his colleagues talked about his fastidiousness. Andy was keen to see what Brian's "let's keep it casual" translated into.

He was surprised. At worst he'd expected chinos pressed to within an inch of the fabric's life, and if not a collar and tie then an expensive polo - Gucci or Galliano maybe - probably accompanied by an impeccably matched blazer or sports jacket. Andy had seen Brian dressed 'smart casual' before. What actually confronted him was a trim, greying man on the very verge of retirement, belying his sixty-five years, wearing a loose college sweatshirt, jeans and Nike trainers.

"Brian, hi," Andy said as he extended his hand.

Brian smiled.

"I said casual, young man..." He'd always been brilliant at reading other people, interpreting a glance, the meaning behind a furrowed brow. Evidently Andy had been completely transparent.

"I just thought..."

"Don't worry about it!" He placed his hand on Andy's right shoulder. "This is me in transition. So I thought, why not take this old sweat for a spin on my last official night? I'll probably be living in it from tomorrow onwards!"

Andy looked at the two big green letters stitched onto the front of the sweatshirt.

"'W' and 'M'?"

"William and Mary, my Alma Mater in Williamsburg, Virginia. This isn't one of the originals I used to wear all those years ago of course, but I like to support them, you know. And they invite me over to give talks from time to time."

"I've heard of Williamsburg, I think."

"Colonial Williamsburg? Very British. You'd love it!"

Andy laughed.

"Shall we?" Brian released the younger man's shoulder and gestured towards the restaurant's open door.

*

"I'm afraid I won't, Andy."

They had just been seated and were looking through the menu. Andy had suggested that, as he would be paying, Brian could go to town if he wanted. After all, hadn't he deserved it?

"I know what they've told you. 'Take the Old Man to that nice Italian place - the one where we have the deal with the Manager, Franco - and just treat him. Whatever he wants. We'll pick up the tab.'" He paused, seeing Andy beginning to smile. "Am I right?"

"Pretty much."

"And about 'the Old Man' thing too, because I know that's what they call me when they think I can't hear."

Andy laughed.

"It's affectionate." He hesitated briefly. "We all do."

Brian nodded.

"Well don't worry, no offence taken. At all. And you should hear what I call some of *them* when they're not listening!"

His laugh was rich and infectious; not in a superficial way but as if it were valuable, suitable, appropriate, because of his experience and the knowledge that lay behind it. When Brian laughed you got the impression he was doing so because it was the right thing to do. It gave you confidence. The guys loved him for that.

"What about me?" Andy asked.

"You?"

"What did you call me behind my back?" It was a playful question, one that Andy would never have dared asking under normal circumstances. But then these weren't normal circumstances: Brian was wearing jeans and a sweatshirt.

"You really want to know?" The older man noticed the change in the tense Andy used. It was a sign that things were at the tipping point. He let it go.

"Sure, why not? If only because then I'll know what the others will be calling me."

"Because they'll have taken my lead?" Andy nodded in reply. "At least two good lessons right there. I can see we made a smart choice."

"Lessons?"

"Don't take yourself *too* seriously; number one. Number two; leadership starts at the top. As the boss, whatever *you* do everyone else picks up on. You can have all the motivational visionary posterised BS you want, but it's what you *do* that counts."

Brian glanced back at the menu. Andy thought it was pretty standard Italianate fare - a bit pricey because it was London, but maybe somewhat better quality that you'd normally enjoy in town. And Franco was a straight enough guy - Andy had met him - he didn't mess you about.

"That spotty English kid," Brian said suddenly.

"Sorry?"

"What I used to call you - at least at first. Of course, you weren't spotty, but you seemed so young - to me, anyway. Don't worry, I don't think the guys picked up on that one!"

Andy laughed.

"Which one *did* they pick up on then?"

"Oh, I don't know. Sancho Panza, probably."

"Who?"

"The guy from 'Don Quixote'. The tilting at windmills one. I've never read it mind, so my reference may be way off. Received wisdom - or semi-popular culture at best maybe. Anyway, that's one of the things I liked about you: never afraid to take something on, try something out. Even when others thought it might be a pipe dream, you had a reputation for giving it a go. So, Sancho Panza and the windmill thing."

"Should I be flattered? I'm not sure." Andy laughed again.

"You should, absolutely. Panza was a really wise guy. It's another reason why I think you're the right man for the job. Prepared to try things out; not paranoid about failure; learns lessons. Happy to take the knocks when things don't work out."

"And some didn't."

"Sure. But how do you know that unless you try? And, by the way, from where I sat most of them *did* work out. Even the ones that went wrong or missed the mark, they moved us forward as a business. We needed that. *You* need that still." He corrected himself. "Having some safe Johnny in the hot seat is the beginning of the end."

Andy thought of Ross, the Texan he had been certain would inherit the mantle from Brian. Ross had been with the company all his working life, knew it inside-out. For most people he was that safe pair of hands; the right kind of person to entrust with Brian's legacy and keep it going. He wanted to know why they hadn't given the job to Ross but wasn't sure how to ask.

✳

"I love gnocchi," Brian said once they had ordered. He had chosen gnocchi in a pesto sauce for his starter. "We just don't do it well enough in the States - at least not in the places I'm used to eating."

"Not with all that Italian ancestry over there?"

"You're right, it's not all Mafia and pizza. I'm sure there are some places in the big cities where you can get good gnocchi; maybe I just haven't found one."

"I went to a great Italian with Ross in Houston once. We were doing the rounds, visiting the service centres, warehouses. It was his home turf, so knew exactly where to go."

"Did they do gnocchi?"

"Can't say for sure, sorry."

"Well he never took *me* anywhere that sounded that good when I was in Houston with him."

There was a slight pause as they took sips from the wine they had ordered; based on Brian's experience, a good white burgundy was also a rarity in the US. It was, he told Andy, going to be his one true indulgence of the evening.

"He's a good guy," Brian suggested, slightly hesitantly.

Andy sensed him fishing.

"I've always liked him. I think we get on well."

"That's good, because you'll need to lean on him. Knows more about the business than anyone - including me."

"That's what I'd thought. To be honest, I thought he'd get the job."

"Your job."

"Yes," Andy smiled. "*Our* job."

Brian raised his glass in recognition of the compliment.

"Ross is a great number two - I love the guy. He was best man at my wedding; my second one, that is. But he'd make a lousy number one. And all he knows is our business. Man and boy. He's got no outside reference points; has nothing to compare us with, no experience of anything external. If you don't have that, you just get more of the same - only less so."

"No Sancho Panza then?"

"Not even close."

❋

"Don't make the same mistakes I did."

The starters had come and gone, the gnocchi broadly living up to Brian's hopes for it. They had chatted idly; a little more about Ross, restaurants in America. He had asked Andy when he next planned to be in the US.

"Mistakes? Surely there weren't many?" Andy asked.

"But there weren't none. And you always make mistakes; everyone does. Or at least things that you see as mistakes because with the benefit of hindsight you can think of better ways of tackling them."

"I agree there, of course. But mistakes?"

"OK," Brian paused, weighing up examples. "I never spent enough time in Europe. Or enough time out of the US. It's a common enough mistake that most Americans make. Lots of us don't really understand the rest of the world very well."

"But you were here in the UK and in Europe regularly. We must have seen you six or eight times a year. That hardly smacks of getting it wrong to me."

"You'll see. It can never be enough. Never. And you'll have the same challenge I did, Andy. You're everyone's CEO; no matter where they are, they all think they have a right to a slice."

"Which is fair enough, isn't it?" Andy asked.

"Sure, sure. But there isn't enough time - isn't enough of you to go around. My advice - if you want it?"

"Please."

"Make a *realistic* plan; let people know about it early - to set expectations; then don't disappoint. Don't say you'll be in Houston four times a year when you know that's going to be a stretch. Say you'll be there twice, and be there twice. If you get the chance to pop in a third time, or fourth, then great. Same story everywhere. Who's your EA?"

"Barbara Wills."

"I know Barbara. Really smart cookie. Have her hook up with Jeanie; she'll be able to tell her where I went wrong with my scheduling, then she'll be able to advise you on what the travelling's really like. Boy, there are some skeletons in my closet when it comes to travel! Stuff I'd planned but never saw through."

"Surely not?"

"You'd be surprised!"

There was an undercurrent in Brian's tone which, for the first time that evening, gave Andy a sense of what the older man was going to miss. Currently, the sweatshirt and jeans were for show, for Andy's benefit; they weren't yet representations of who Brian was going to be next.

"What else? What other mistakes?"

"How long have you got?" They both laughed. "Early days? Thinking I knew it all, had all the answers. Wanting to do things to make my mark, to prove that I was in charge. All that Alpha Male type stuff. It's all crap really. Window dressing at best. Actually that's an area where Ross can help. Bounce ideas off him; he has a pretty good radar, and he'll tell you when you're just plain wrong."

"Which may be quite a lot of the time in the early days."

"It *will* be quite a lot of the time," Brian agreed. "I didn't see that. And I didn't see until a while later that the way you become good at this job is by increasing the contribution that everyone else makes. That's how to make an impact. Look for people who can do more, who want to impress, who have talent, ideas, vision. Give some of them an early boost, a chance; they'll love you for it."

Andy allowed a slight pause as he took another sip of wine.

"So who will you miss then, Brian?"

"People-wise?"

Andy nodded.

"In addition to Jeanie and Ross? I don't know. Just about everyone I guess. When they start to feel like family, then you know you're beginning to do the job right."

＊

For the rest of the meal they alternated between work and non-work topics. Andy wanted to get as much from Brian as he could, yet didn't want to overwhelm him - and it was Brian's show anyway; he could talk about anything he liked. Occasionally they tried to steer away from the company and tiptoed into safe subjects like sport, holidays, family; but here the conversation became a little forced. It was as if there was a formula to which they were trying to adhere, a convention for meals when guys were just supposed to be 'shooting the breeze'; but Brian only came alive when he was able to find a way of diverting their various threads back to the business.

So a conversation on beer and the merits and demerits of US craft ale led on to the 'Cheers' TV show, from there into a discussion about Boston, and then - having established the geographic location - the challenges for the company's plant just outside Foxborough, and the plans for redevelopment there. It was one of many as yet unfinished initiatives that had been Brian's baby. Andy could see his fingerprints across the business and, in doing so, realised that just changing the nameplate on the door of 'the corner office' didn't mean he would be in charge right away. The transition would carry on long after Brian had left the building. Loyalty didn't transfer automatically; Andy knew he would have to earn that.

But as he listened to Brian talking about how he had arrived at his decision with regard to Foxborough (it had been an 'invest-or-close' binary choice), Andy knew that taking the company out of Brian would be harder than extracting Brian from the company. He knew Brian would never walk away emotionally; he would be a company man as long as he breathed, and Andy found himself envying that - even wondering if in twenty years time he might be in the same position.

It was a romantic notion. As hard as he might find it to step up, it would be many times harder for Brian to step out. The sweatshirt fooled no-one.

"You'll have to keep a close eye on that one," Brian was telling him. "Greg's a good guy and it should be fine, but the business case is a little tight and so any slippage won't be great."

Brian looked up from his espresso to find a slight smile on Andy's face. He nodded slightly, more to himself than anyone else.

"I know, I know. You don't have to say anything."

"About what?"

"About how tough it's going to be letting go."

"You'll be checking the share price every day, thinking 'What's that idiot Andrew up to?'!"

Brian laughed.

"Well, the first part's probably right, at least."

He finished his coffee and allowed himself a slow glance around the restaurant. Andy recognised it as one of those 'last time I'll be here' kind of looks. He could almost hear doors starting to close.

*

They paused outside the hotel.

"I know guys," Brian began, "who spend their lives looking forward to this day; the day when you can draw a line under work, of doing something for someone else. They imagine what the new dawn will bring them, the freedom it represents; they think that it will be great being able to get up at whatever time they want in the mornings, not to have to go to meetings, to spend quality time with their families."

"And won't it be? Won't all those things be good?"

"Sure. But if you've worked as much for yourself as you have for a business then you realise that you've been free enough all along. At least that's what I think. I did as much in my job for me as for the company." He paused. "That makes me lucky, I guess."

"And it probably helped make you great at what you did."

Brian sighed. To Andy, he suddenly seemed as if he had shrunk a little; as if the man he was leaving on the steps of the hotel was somehow not the same man he had met outside the restaurant just a couple of hours ago.

At some imperceptible sign, they both glanced down and extended their right hands forward.

"I guess we're both a little nervous right now," Brian said as he released the younger man's grip. "The safety net's gone. Come Monday that office is yours. When you look up, you won't see anyone there any more." He laughed, sharply. "And when I look down, I won't see anyone there either..."

A Walk in Roundhay Park

As the blue Audi cabriolet pulled to a halt in the car park, Pat, sitting on a bench near the entrance to the cafe, didn't need to look at his watch to verify how late Andy was; he'd been checking it on-and-off for the last forty minutes.

The man who emerged from the car, mobile phone pressed to his left ear, gave a wave and a slight shrug of the shoulders. It was a gesture that simultaneously said "Sorry, pal", "Not my fault!", "You know how it is…". Pat wasn't surprised his old friend was as late as this. Driving towards the park from Roundhay Road he'd had a bet with himself as to how late Andy would be. He'd gone for fifteen-to-thirty minutes. Obviously that was a tad optimistic these days. As Pat stood and walked back to the car park, he couldn't fail to recall when it would have been a shock for Andy to have been fifteen- or thirty-*seconds* late! The last four years had taken their toll - and in more ways than just time-keeping.

Pat was no more than four steps away from Andy when he finally lowered the phone.

"Busy?" Pat suggested unnecessarily, offering his hand.

Andy shook it warmly as he simultaneously dropped the phone into the inside pocket of his jacket.

"You know what these Scandinavians are like," he said rhetorically, "always another question that needs answering, something else needing to be clarified."

Pat laughed.

"Not all Scandinavians, surely?"

"You're right. Probably only the ones I have to work with."

They fell into step without thinking about it, heading past the bench on which Pat had recently been sitting and towards the lake.

"Coffee first or second?" Andy asked.

"Second, I think. I'd like to kid myself I've earned it for a change."

Andy took in the full length of his friend.

"Not running so much these days?"

"Not so much. That obvious is it?"

"Life can be a little cruel when you get to our age. There always seem to be more and more reasons why we can't find the time to do the things we used to."

"Including Scandinavians," Pat suggested.

If you had looked of them perhaps fifteen years earlier, you would have seen slightly slimmer versions of their present day selves. Little else would have been materially different, at least from a distance. From that perspective, time had been relatively kind.

They would probably have been running too. Young men out for their weekend exercise, atoning for a late night or recharging the batteries in preparation for another week at work. Although Andy had been moving ahead professionally, when they were in their running gear it was Pat who always had the edge. If you were to ask, neither would admit to ever having raced the other, though the truth was that Andy always tried to finish in front at the end of their run - and that Pat was never going to let him. Each being slightly ahead of the other in different spheres - work and play, if you like - gave their relationship an equilibrium. It was a balance they maintained all through their university days and on into the world of work where - as coincidence would have it - they ended up working for the same company for a while.

"How long has it been?" Pat asked.

"Since what?"

"Since we went round the lake together? Six years?"

"Longer," Andy replied. "I left Leeds ten years ago when I got that promotion to London."

"Ten years? That's something. And look at you now…"

"Fat and flabby?" Andy laughed. "But if you want to run round Pat, you just let me know!"

Pat treated it as the bluff and bluster it was, but he also knew that if he'd taken up Andy's offer, they would have been off and away even in their heavy shoes and winter coats.

As they turned left past the cafe entrance and began to walk towards the far end of the lake they did so in silence. The path was well trodden here and recent rain had resulted in the presence of a number of puddles and patches of mud. Navigation seemed to require silence.

"It amazes me that they've never sorted this path out," Andy said as soon as they had been able to walk side-by-side again. "The smallest drop of rain and it gets like this."

"It'll be worse at the far end - as always."

For a split second there was the hint that they might not try and walk round the lake after all but rather retrace their steps immediately and give in to the lure of coffee and cake. But then the moment was gone, displaced by the sight of a mum ahead of them who had paused to retrieve the small teddy which had fallen from her child's buggy and was now in serious need of a wash. Pat went ahead as they reverted to single file for a moment.

"How is Leeds? Same as ever?"

Andy's question, carried through the air, caught Pat up before the speaker did.

"Same as," he replied, once they were in stride again. "The odd new building in the centre of town - mainly flats - and the odd old business relocating here."

"They tell me at the office that the city's booming, northern financial hub and all that."

"So they say."

"It's a shame I haven't been able to get up here much; not as much as I used to anyway. And that's not just the fault of the Scandinavians, before you say anything!"

"I think the fact that the last three times we met were all in London speaks volumes."

"Meaning?"

"You. Your work. Big important man now. Globe trotting executive. Keeping the wheels of commerce moving. Needing to be at the centre of things. Which - let's face it - isn't Leeds."

"Not in the context of my business, no; but other companies, surely? Your outfit's doing okay, isn't it?"

They were walking alongside some threadbare bushes to their right, a short stretch where the path did not directly butt up against the lake. Pat waited until they were in plain sight of the water again before replying, almost as if there might be someone hiding in the bushes trying to listen in on their conversation.

"Growing slowly. Nothing spectacular."

"The share price seems pretty solid."

"You checked our share price?!" Pat's voice carried a note of surprise blended in with a tone which betrayed he knew Andy would do that.

"Force of habit, I guess."

"I saw you've just bought out one of your competitors."

"The gig in Manchester?"

Pat nodded.

"No brainer, really. And we got a good deal, too. Fits perfectly with our strategy and where we're trying to get to. 'Another brick in the wall' as one of the team said to me the other day."

"Or a brick in the Yellow Brick Road."

Andy laughed.

In their university days they'd had a soft spot for 'The Wizard of Oz', and when drunk used to argue over the merits and demerits of the film and which character each of them could play. In the main it had been light-hearted, alcohol-induced stuff. Andy had Pat pegged as the Cowardly Lion, and had once used his refusal to move away from the city to try something more adventurous as proof of this theory. Indeed, it was a parallel that had resurfaced when they had briefly met in London a few months earlier. Pat had always seen Andy as some kind of Tin Man - though for no blatantly obvious reason. More recently however it felt to Pat as if his profile had shifted more toward the Wicked Witch of the West. He had said nothing of course.

"Let's kidnap Toto!"

It had been a standing joke. They had argued that if the dog went missing, the film simply couldn't exist. The tomfoolery of youth, Pat knew, but he had begun to wonder if - given half the chance - the present day Andy might just have carried out the threat.

A false step on a patch of mud threw Pat, leaving him momentarily off balance.

"Watch yourself there," he warned over his shoulder, Andy having dropped into single file behind him again as the state of the path worsened. When there was no response, he glanced behind him. Andy was stationery, mobile phone in his hand once more, his eyes fixed on its screen.

It was a pose which jarred with their surroundings; not with the park so much - after all, these days you couldn't go anywhere without seeing people buried in their private yet paradoxically connected worlds - but for Pat walking around Roundhay Park with Andy still represented a symbol of their youth, a shared past. It was, even if only in some tangental way, a statement about who they had been, both individually and together. Andy, in instantly absenting himself like this, lured away by a 'ping' from his jacket pocket, seemed to be making a statement about values with which Pat struggled. He knew how significant Andy's job was, and could only guess at the pressures and demands of being the CEO of a global business. You were, he assumed, at everyone's beck and call - which was ironic, because most people would automatically believe it was the other way round. But the fact that Andy could make that switch - and so readily, too - when they were having some private time on a Sunday morning, made Pat feel as if their friendship had been demoted, that he had been devalued. His shares - in Andy's terminology - had fallen.

His invitation for Andy to join him on a walk round the lake - "for old time's sake" - had been made as soon as he had discovered he was going to be in Leeds for a couple of days, attending some industry 'bash' on the Saturday night. To promote his case he had pulled all the emotional strings he had at his disposal. Over the previous three years - ever since that stratospheric promotion - Pat had watch his friend gradually change. Not that he was surprised by this, not really; after all, how can you be elevated to such a level and take on so much responsibility without needing to adjust? Pat had assumed that much of the change would be seen in disciplines, working practices, an alteration in focus or prioritisation; things like that. He had taken for granted that the core of who you were would remain intact, unsullied by such new pressures. Perhaps that was because he hoped that's how he'd behave under similar circumstances. But he had sensed - and then seen - Andy's new reality beginning to impinge. Even during those short coffee-bar get-togethers in London it had begun to feel as if his friend was re-evaluating his own past given he had a new set of imperatives within which to operate. This vague sense had prompted him to see if he could find a way to validate his assessment. Was he imagining things or was Andy really a changed person? Roundhay Park represented something of a datum point for Pat. It was base camp; something almost elemental in their relationship. The walk was his way of stress-testing who they still were.

"Italians this time?" Pat suggested as Andy, freed from his phone rejoined him.

"On a Sunday?!"

"OK, maybe not."

They continued walking for a few steps in silence.

"So how is it? Really. The new job I mean?"

"Great. Just great." Andy looked across. "But you asked me that before, in London. At least twice."

"Did I? Well then." Pat paused, then picked up the thread again. "But that would have been when you didn't really know, wouldn't it? I mean, in the early days - with all the euphoria and newness of it - how could it be anything other? But now? Now that the excitement has worn off... I just wondered if it was still 'great'."

On the lake a number of round wooden poles poked through the surface of the water and rose some three feet above it. Seagulls used these remnants from an earlier jetty - now long since disappeared - as outposts where they would sit and watch. Andy allowed his gaze to wander to a solitary bird on the penultimate post, and let it rest there another second or two before responding.

"I'd say so, yes. But it's a different kind of great now, of course. But isn't that like any job? At the interview it's one thing; on day one it's something else; on day four hundred... It has to change."

"And change us too?"

"I'm not making as many mistakes now, that's for sure."

"Mistakes?"

"Brian - the guy before me - he said I'd make mistakes and he was right. I probably even made exactly the same mistakes he did! But no harm done, eh?"

"That's good."

"Nothing major anyway," Andy offered a smile that verged on the conspiratorial. Pat knew he was joking.

"A few pence on the share price? Perhaps some unhappy Scandinavians?"

"Something like that." Andy's attention was caught by the seagull which had decided to take to the wing.

"But I'm interested: do you change the job, or does the job change you? If you assume it's not a perfect fit from day one, that is. And making mistakes surely suggests it can't have been."

They were turning at the top end of the lake. The concrete path had given way to a rough and muddy track that ran through some trees for a few yards. Once again they were in single file, concentrating on avoiding the grey-brown puddles, uncertain how deep some of them might have been; traps for the unwary.

"What do you think?" Andy eventually replied, countering Pat's question with one of his own.

"Me? I don't know. I guess in my limited experience - and considering the level at which I work - the job is the job. You get very little chance to change it, not really; so you have to mould yourself around it."

"At your level? You do yourself down!"

"You know what I mean. But for you; well, you can change all the jobs if you want to, can't you? You're in charge, after all."

"Always looking down."

"What?"

"Sorry. Something else Brian said." Andy paused. "I suppose it is different. And you're right, after a couple of years you do get a better handle on things; you get to know really what's going on and what you need to do to be successful."

"At any cost?"

They were side-by-side again, having just moved to the side to allow two joggers to run by them.

"That's an interesting choice of phrase, Pat. And loaded too. What's on your mind?"

Pat had rehearsed their conversation, estimated when they would need to have finished with the pleasantries and got onto the meat of the subject - at least from his perspective. The round poles were immediately to their right now and the seagull had returned to its station.

"Just an observation, that's all."

"About me?"

"Or about the job, I suppose. I was trying to gauge."

Andy paused for a split second.

"But it can't be about the job. You don't know the job. You can't interrogate the job. Therefore it must be about me."

There was a tone in Andy's voice Pat was keen to dispel.

"I just wondered if you felt the job had changed you in any way. Whether there was any kind of knock-on from suddenly having all that responsibility..."

"All that pressure?" Andy suggested.

"Something like that."

Pat sensed his approach had been a little clumsy, but the genii was out of the bottle now.

"Do you think it's changed me?"

"I don't know."

Andy's laugh was short but not unfriendly.

"Come on, Pat; you know me better than almost anyone else. Certainly outside of the business. You're not tainted by the enforced loyalty working together brings. I've known you almost longer than my little brother, for Christ's sake! We've thrown up together in the same bushes!"

It was Pat's turn to laugh.

"Once not a million miles from here, if my memory serves…"

There was a short hiatus. A second seagull swooped across the water and joined the first, alighting on the furthest post. For a moment the two birds eyed each other and then turned their collective gaze back down the lake. A brief gust rippled the surface of the water a little more.

"Well?"

Pat could tell Andy wasn't going to give this up.

"Honest answer?"

"Nothing less."

From Pat's perspective, there was proof right here.

"Why are you smiling? What's funny?"

"Nothing, Andy; nothing at all. Once upon a time you used to let things go; let them slide if they didn't immediately get resolved. I used to think it was quaint in a way, the shortness of your attention span. If you weren't immediately satisfied, you'd move on to the next thing."

"That doesn't sound like me," Andy objected.

"No it doesn't. Not the you of today. But all those years ago?" Pat laughed just a little. "Diana saw it."

"Diana?"

"She said you had no staying power, no focus. That's why she finished with you; because she needed more attention. She required more work than you were prepared to put in."

"She said that?"

Pat nodded.

"You'd know, of course."

"But today's Andy's not like that at all." Pat moved on, refusing to be deflected. "I agree completely. Your focus is totally different. I assume it has to be - because of the job. So you can't abide loose ends like you used to; can't leave things unresolved."

It was Andy's turn to laugh.

"Guilty as charged! But that's how it has to be now."

"Undoubtedly. And my point exactly. That's why I asked the question about the job; how it might have changed you."

They walked on in silence for a few yards.

"But your point is also something else, isn't it? It's not just that I'm a more focussed individual now because I have to be. I can sense you think it's not just that. I think that's another way the job's changed me, if you like; I need to be able to read people better, to get through all the crap on the surface and down to what's really bothering them, to what's important. And I need to do it quickly."

"No dancing round handbags?"

"I gave up handbag-dancing ages ago!"

"And that's a good thing?"

"I think so. In the main, anyway."

"Do you also think then - ignoring all the handbags - that what's important to you has changed? I'm not talking about work. I'm guessing that it's inevitable that the things you have to focus on at work are different today than, say, four or five years ago. Is that fair?"

"That's fair."

"So let's take that as a given. What about outside of work? Or work versus non-work, if you'd prefer?"

"Versus?"

"The choices you make."

"Help me out. Give me a for instance."

Although Pat didn't use it as an example, even this conversation demonstrated how Andy was different. A few years previously he would never had been able to talk about himself for so long. Pat hadn't thought of this until now, just as he dropped behind his friend to let another pair of joggers go by them.

"Okay, an example. How about running?"

"Running?"

"You still run, right?"

"Sure; not as much as I used to. Probably a bit like you, eh?"

Pat inclined his head slightly in acknowledgement.

"It used to take something truly significant to deflect you from your run, if you'd had one planned. What about now?"

Andy laughed.

"That's crazy!"

"Crazy?"

"Crazy. Because, one, we get older. Two, other things intrude on our time. Three, priorities change. That's just growing up, Pat! You'll have to do better than that! If that's my crime, then guilty again."

"All right. How about the Church? You used to disappear every Sunday morning for the early service come rain or shine. What about now?"

Andy remained silent.

"The growing up card?" Pat suggested, keeping a smile close to his lips to try and ensure Andy realised at least part of the interrogation was playful.

"Probably. Thought that's more complex isn't it? Obviously."

"Okay, let's not go there. Sorry."

He paused. At the heart of Pat's concern was the people question, and his belief that Andy wasn't the same friend he had once been. Some of their mutual acquaintances had remarked that Andy had 'dropped off the radar', or had been a little short with them the last time they had spoken. He knew circumstance played a part in all interchanges, but the mounting evidence - even if it was hearsay - was undeniable.

Having mentally envisaged a red line, Pat knew that any further pursuit of his theme could only be another step towards it. Or even beyond. In a way, he had found out what he wanted to know, affirmed his suspicions. Having done so, it was now his issue to deal with, not Andy's. If he had harboured any ambition to prompt change, to turn the tide or have his friend 'see the light', he realised now how naïve a notion that had been. Naïvety was a trait of his own that he hadn't managed to shed.

"So? What else?"

They had turned the corner and were walking along the top of the dam-like wall at the western end of the lake. In a few yards there would be another right turn and then the final short stretch back towards the car park and the cafe.

"You know, it doesn't matter. Let's leave it."

"Leave it? Come on, Pat. How long have we known each other? There's something else. I know there is."

"Well if there is, then maybe it's me," Pat offered. "We've demonstrated you've changed - 'grown up', if you like - and that some of it is down to the job. Fair enough. But maybe there's a part of what I think that's actually down to *me* not changing; to me being pretty much the same as I always have been."

The lack of immediate response was proof enough that Andy was considering this thread seriously. Pat hadn't had any intention of opening himself up to scrutiny. He knew that would not go well. When they were both young, naive, idealistic, innocent, daft - that was a different matter. But now they weren't. Or Andy certainly wasn't. He had thought the issue was solely with his high-flying friend, but maybe not.

He didn't want to find out.

"'What I think'; that's what you said," Andy eventually came back. "Well, what *do* you think, Pat? We've established that there's part of me that's changed, and that inevitably it's down to the job. I've agreed that there are different pressures and priorities, that choices have to be made, that outcomes are different now. All agreed. Guilty, like I said. But it occurs to me that I still don't know what you really think."

"Does it matter?"

"It clearly matters to you or you wouldn't have raised it. I'm not the one dancing around the handbags here…"

The buzzing from Andy's jacket pocket broke into his sentence and he paused to retrieve his phone. Pat carried on walking as soon as he heard Andy's voice, his professional voice.

As they neared the cafe the path became a little busier. Young couples with children in and out of buggies; boys poking at the earth with sticks they had found or swishing them through the rough grass at the path's edge. Dogs on leads of various lengths, sniffing and padding, weaving across the tarmac. And again joggers - this time a singleton nipping past them - running around the lake. He used to know the precise distance of the perimeter, but now couldn't remember it. He glanced over his shoulder; Andy was still talking.

"That went well" he told himself as he reached the car park, a car park that was probably twice as full as when they'd left it. He could see through its windows that the cafe was busier now. There were one or two tables that were free, but it wouldn't be quiet.

He stopped, finding himself mid-way between Andy's car and the entrance to the cafe. Turning, he saw Andy making a hurried remark and then sliding the phone away again. There was a frown on his face.

"How far is it," Pat asked, "around the lake, I mean? Can you remember? I used to know."

"About a mile and a half, I think. Maybe just over. Used to take us eleven or twelve minutes or so. I'm surprised you don't remember. You used to keep some kind of log didn't you?"

Pat remembered the little notebook. Who knows, he probably still had it, lost in the bottom of a box somewhere.

"Before I grew up," he suggested. Then after a pause, "Coffee?"

Andy shook his head, glancing down to where his phone now lay out of sight.

"Sorry, pal. The Scandinavians again. I have to go back to the hotel and get something sorted out."

Pat nodded.

"I understand," he said, even though he still didn't.

Andy was already heading towards his car.

"Bet you couldn't do it in twelve minutes now!"

Pat knew that was true.

He watched the Audi's lights flash and Andy open the door. There was a pause before the engine started, then another delay as the roof began to retract. Pat looked up. The sun was out, but the sky was far from cloudless; there was a chill in the air that he'd forgotten, the mild exertion of their walk insulating him from it. Hardly top-down weather, at least from his perspective.

Andy raised his arm as he wheeled away, shouting something that was drowned out by tyres on gravel, the shouts of children, and the barking of dogs.

They hadn't shaken hands goodbye.

Snow and the Snow Globe

It had been snowing when they first met her. A light inconsequential kind of snow hardly worth the name. A drizzle slightly more solid than usual; precipitation hitting the ground then thinking for a moment before deciding that trying to remain there was too much effort. It would have another go at some other point in time and in some other place. The weather had been obtuse in any event. Just two weeks previously they had been able to wear t-shirts - t-shirts in November!

They had seen her around the place, of course; she and her two friends were seldom apart. "They hunt in a pack" someone said to him one day as he watched the triumvirate sashay out of the refectory. It was a comment born of jealousy and reputation, like a virus which infected all the young men who wanted to get close to them but knew they couldn't; couldn't because they weren't smart enough, or handsome enough, interesting or rich enough. Many simply weren't old or experienced enough.

It was an unkind appellation, but they were known as 'The Three Witches'. If pressed, no-one could say why. Being slim, blonde (with the assistance of certain potions in one case) and of above-average attractiveness were certainly not the normal characteristics associated with witches. Broomsticks and Black Cats they were not. Their female contemporaries had other words for the cohort too; derogatory terms arising from a different perspective - but still a swathed in jealousy nonetheless.

Few people seemed to really know or be friendly with them. They added gloss; a gilding that made the things they touched more lustrous - but it was a veneer which did not reward too much scrutiny.

That, at least, was the popular view.

Patrick had no idea what Diana saw in Andy. Taking their supposed qualification criteria into account - intelligence, good looks, wealth, charisma - he felt his friend was middling at best. He couldn't speak definitively with regard to Andy's family background - and thus the presence or absence of 'wealth' - but all the indications were that he was as 'normal' as anyone else. What had piqued Diana's interest that fateful, snowy November day neither Patrick nor Andy were able to say. It had been an accidental coming together in Borders; the tumbling of a few books, an unguarded profanity, a risqué joke, an invitation to coffee once the brief laughter had subsided. That something had passed between them, invisibly and within touching distance, was undeniable - as was Diana's presence at breakfast in Andy's campus flat the following morning, its other occupants tingling at the surprise of it all.

If it felt like a coup, Andy never let on. He played down the enormity of the event - one of 'The Three Witches' sleeping in *his* bed! - and, to his credit, he treated Diana in the same way he had his previous two girlfriends. Unlike most of his friends, his avoiding any semblance of being 'star struck' seemed more of a triumph than the fact of her being there at all. Yet even though Patrick came to know Diana peripherally in those early days, an acquaintance gifted through their shared relationship with Andy, it didn't take him long to realise that unless Andy 'upped his game', Diana's presence would be fleeting.

And so it proved. There were certain 'rules' that Diana was keen to apply to their arrangement; preconditions to ensure Andy remained entitled to stay in the game. It was soon clear that either Andy didn't understand this obligation or he was too ambivalent to really care. The inevitable consequence was that Diana's admittedly few kitchen appearances ceased almost as soon as they had begun.

Strangely, Patrick's insight into what had happened came not from his best friend, but from Diana herself.

He had been sitting in a corner of the vaulted library hall surrounded by dark panelling, shelves filled with a blur of books, and the murmurs of whispered conversations that weren't supposed to be happening at all. Although the open hardbacks and sheets of hand-written A4 lying in front of him suggested otherwise, he was stuck. Being stuck didn't mean that he wasn't engrossed, however, and it took a repetition of "Hi" from his right to alert him to Diana's presence.

"You look busy," she offered unnecessarily, rotating the book nearest her so that she could make out its topic. "Tudor history? Nice."

"Not right now it's not," he replied, slightly thrown by her being there, talking to him.

"I can go away if you want."

"No, please don't. It's fine."

Her distraction was welcome, and not just because it dragged him away from the early Henrys. At a superficial level, there was a certain caché in being seen talking with a Witch one-to-one, and Patrick couldn't help but glance up to see who nearby had noticed. He was also intrigued as to why she was there at all. The denouement with Andy had occurred around a week previously, and Patrick's not illogical assumption was that event also heralded the last he would see of her, at least in close proximity.

She smiled and in doing so surfaced the third reason he was glad she was there: he actually liked her. He had never tried to rationalise whether this was because he found her a genuinely okay individual, or because he had become mildly besotted with her via the brief and somewhat tangential access he had enjoyed courtesy of Andy.

"I just wanted to try and understand what it was with Andy. I mean, why did he behave like he did?"

With little difficulty she had dragged him away from Aubrey's 'Brief Lives' to the second, smaller refectory buried deep in the Union building. Having a reputation for being the home of the 'in crowd', it was an environment in which he rarely trespassed - though it was, of course, no surprise that was where Diana gravitated.

"In what way?" Patrick found himself looking up, just as he had in the library, to gauge who might be interested in their presence - though in this case, *he* was the interloper.

"Like he didn't care. I liked him," - Patrick noticed the tense - "and so was a little disappointed."

She had hesitated sufficiently over the last word for him to know that wasn't what she truly meant, so he applied his own interpretation and moved on.

"Because that's a bit how he is," Patrick suggested. "He's 'relaxed'." He applied the parentheses as clearly as he could. "There are some things about which he isn't relaxed; where he's obsessed, passionate, unwavering if you like - but I don't think girls fall in to that category. Not yet at least. Or not that I've seen."

He waited for her to respond, for a moment fixing on her eyes - a blue he had never realised was totally stunning until now - before averting his gaze and carrying on.

"So it's not you. How could it be?" He let the question hang unintentionally for a moment. "I don't know. It's a question of - priorities."

He looked up again. Her gaze had not left him.

"You're sure? Sure that it wasn't me, or something I'd done? I'm not stupid - or deaf. I know what people say sometimes. That's not how I am, not really." It was her turn to look away. "It can be - difficult."

"How could it be you?" He repeated, rhetorically.

She looked back at him and smiled, her hand giving his arm a light squeeze.

"Promise?"

"Promise."

Sitting at the kitchen table looking out into the garden, it had been the snow that had in part prompted the memory. Unlike that November of a few years ago, this snow consisted of large, delicate and distinct flakes that floated to earth casually; flakes certain in the knowledge they would land and remain where they fell. It was mid-winter after all and the bad weather had been expected. Although it hadn't been the first time he had seen snow in the last few years, the memory was not one he replayed regularly. If not simply snow then, could Patrick say what else had triggered it? Perhaps silence.

He had always felt that snow brought silence. In settling like a white blanket over things, it absorbed sound, deadened it, creating a strange acoustic magic trick that swallowed noise. Being in the house alone, it was the kind of effect he now felt; all ambient noises had vanished when she left. The only ones that remained were those he made. It was as if a different kind of blanket had been laid over the roof.

Silence and snow. And the painful proximity of recent events. Those were his triggers.

After that short refectory chat, Diana sought him out ever more frequently. It had been a surreal experience for Patrick, at least initially; the notion that he possessed an intrinsic value - for her of all people! - was difficult to rationalise. Once, when he had managed to ask (in a roundabout way!) why she was still engaging with him, she had told him that he was a good listener.

"And you don't judge me," she'd said. "You're neutral, honest. A sounding board I can trust. Most of my other friends are not like that. They can be a little shallow at times - am I allowed to say that? - and maybe don't always have my best interests at heart."

"And I do?"

"You tell it like it is; I can rely on you giving me a realistic perspective. You're dispassionate; you have no hidden agenda."

Of course *dis*-passionate was the last thing Patrick quickly became. Each time they met he fell increasingly under Diana's spell. How could he not? And with this falling came burgeoning desire. It was - to use her own words - a 'hidden agenda' that remained exactly that. It had to. And during those last two years at University, he moulded himself into what Diana needed him to be. Unlike Andy, who simply couldn't do so - or who didn't care enough to make the effort - Patrick could. And largely because he *did* care enough.

By Easter in their final year they were meeting almost daily, always adhering to a regular pattern: she seeking him out or making the arrangement to meet; he attentive, listening, offering advice. He had established an internal equilibrium too;

one that held his passion and ambition in check; one knowing that spending time with Diana in such a way, on her terms, was infinitely preferable to not seeing her at all.

And then one day she had simply kissed him.

As he recalled it now in his snow-bound kitchen, it still forced a smile to his lips - in spite of the pain of their recent scene. He knew he had been completely thrown, his world suddenly turned on its head. He had felt as if he had been living inside a snow-globe, and that Diana had just picked it up and given it a shake. She had laughed when she saw the shock on his face. She grabbed one of his arms with both her hands and pulled herself against him. She had called him a "stupid idiot" and then kissed him again.

Three years later - and just three weeks ago - she had stood in the kitchen, almost exactly where he was seated now, and shouted at him.

"What the hell am I doing here?! What did I ever see in you?"

Unable to provide her with an immediate answer, he remained silent. She had flung her empty coffee cup into the sink, walked out of the kitchen and, while he remained stationary, grabbed her coat from the hall stand and left. When he got back from work the next day most of her things were gone.

The silence had started to descend at that point, as if someone had finally turned off a tap that had been dripping; dripping for so long he had eventually failed to notice it - that is, until its persistent beat was missing. As he cleared up the smashed pieces of crockery, he heard Andy's voice in his head.

"What?!" he had exclaimed on hearing that Diana had moved in with him. "It will never last. Are you a complete idiot? How? Why? I mean, sorry, but isn't she just a little bit out of your league?"

Patrick hadn't been offended. How could he have been, given he was as surprised as his friend?

"I know, I know - and thanks for the support, by the way! Don't think I haven't asked myself the same questions. I haven't any answers either. I'm crazy about her, of course; I mean, how can you not be? She said I make her feel comfortable, safe, happy."

"'Comfortable'? What the fuck's that supposed to mean?"

Of course Patrick didn't really know. Those two months after Easter were a maelstrom of Diana and examinations; every day she seemed to shake the snow globe again, just to keep him on his toes. She moved in with him in May, and then when the exams were over simply said "Where do we go next?"

They agreed they would go wherever their first job took them. It seemed that might be Edinburgh when he began to close in on a junior role with a consultancy firm there; then, just as they were getting to final interview stage, Diana landed something lucrative in an Ad Agency right there in Leeds. So they ended up going nowhere, at least geographically. They changed flats a couple of times, then found the house in Chapel Allerton.

The snow globe had stopped shaking. For a while at least.

He couldn't help himself and looked back for triggers, for the signs that should have warned him and red-flagged his future. Seeing Diana happy and enthusiastic in her new job, Patrick did what he had always done, ever since she had said "Hi" in the library: he put himself second. Internally, he liked to portray himself as being caring, considerate, selfless; he wanted to see it as his natural persona. Indeed, to a great extent it was; he was not a pushy, egotistical individual. He told himself playing second fiddle was a role to which he was suited. It had worked with Andy. It suited the junior nature of the job he eventually found in Leeds with a solid, family run firm that got his career off the ground; the same company that Andy had joined and briefly blazed through before blasting off on a career Patrick knew would one day be stratospheric. Given that as a yardstick, he thought his approach was a formula that worked.

Yet all the while, Diana had started to move in a different orbit. Her colleagues were creative, lively, risk-taking; they liked adventure, pushing the boundaries. She would return home and tell him of their latest success or their next venture. When there were parties or evenings out, initially she invited

Patrick along but gradually stopped doing so. One day he realised he had failed to notice. "Comfortable, safe, happy" was the mantra he kept coming back to. That was his role, to be that. He thought stability, reliability and predictability were the keys, so while Diana changed, he remained static, the same person she had pulled from the library and taken for a coffee.

Which was not what she wanted any more.

"Christ, you're so boring! You never want to *do* anything."

That had been part of the outburst, the shockwave to destroy his house of cards. Although the explosion had been a sudden one, he now knew it was simply the manifestation of a cancer that been a long time growing. What had been the tipping point? He didn't know. Either he couldn't see it, or he was spoiled for choice.

She had talked about taking some time out and going to South America for a few months. One of her colleagues had just done something similar in the Far East and her firm encouraged such short sabbaticals. Without consulting him, she had acquired a small tattoo on her right ankle; had dyed her hair a somewhat racy shade of auburn; had stopped wearing a bra to work. She had started working longer hours; volunteered to go away on weekend conferences; traded up her small, safe car for a sporty two-door coupe that Patrick had mistakenly suggested she might struggle to drive - and which she couldn't really afford anyway.

"One day," Andy had warned him, "the Witch will come back."

Patrick wasn't sure that was true. His loyalty - and what he supposed was his love for her - prevented him from seeing it that way. Over the previous few days he had tried to exorcise his feeling for her, but could not; he had tried to relocate himself in his own history and insert the 'remodelled' Diana into that framework. If this new, bra-less, tattooed individual had said "Hi" to him in the library, what would he have done?

It was a specious argument; the new Diana would never have sought him out.

He stood up and walked to the window. On the small lawn outside, the snow was probably already two centimetres or so deep. The sky, previously a leaden yellow, was beginning to change its hue, and the flakes were falling less profusely now. As soon as it had stopped he would go and clear the path down to the front gate, then start making his tea. He owed Andy a phone call. Perhaps today was the day to let him know what had happened.

A Tolerable Answer

(February 2016)

"Where did we get to? Let's see. Here it is, page eighty-seven. Oh yes, I remember; Elizabeth has spent the night at Jane's beside. A kind of vigil, I suppose. Which is apt, isn't it? Just let me know if you disagree.

"Didn't I say that last time? Probably, knowing me.

"Do you mind if we don't get into it straight away? I'm not sure I'm quite in the mood just yet; not after what the Doctor's just told me. Did they tell you? They should have; that's what I think. But maybe under the circumstances… And they're so busy. Perhaps saving a few minutes here and there makes all the difference.

"So, should I tell you what they told me? You have a right to know, even when the news isn't great.

"Anyway, they've got the results back from the tests they did yesterday. I didn't ask what tests, exactly; no point them telling me, is there? I've given up pretending to understand. I'm sure they'll explain it in full to Sharon when she comes in this afternoon, after all she's the one who really needs to know; who has the right to know. They don't have to tell me anything, do they? But they've seen me often enough. Eighty-seven pages of enough! Friend of the family and all that. I think that Doctor Walsh - you know, the one with the lovely wavy hair - I think he has a bit of a soft spot for me, and it was him I spoke to. He's very 'simpatico'; isn't that what they say?

"And he's got a great manner; the way he smiles softly and caringly, even when he's delivering the worst possible news. I guess they're all trained to do that - but he seems particularly good at it. I hope he hasn't had too much practice. I would imagine that kind of thing would wear you away after a time…

"Sorry, Jack; I'm procrastinating.

"The headline news is that it won't be long now. Not very long at all. I'm sure Sharon won't be surprised, but even so… It'll probably hit her like a train. Should I stay around, do you think? Would it be helpful if I were here when they told her? I know I'm the last person whose shoulder she would want to cry on, but maybe just this once we might be able to cease hostilities. Or - and I hope you don't mind me saying this - *she* might cease hostilities, because it's pretty much all on her side. You know that don't you? I've never had anything against her. Not personally. Other than jealousy, of course!

"Maybe that's what made her hostile; my jealousy. Saw it as a threat. Being worried that one day I might try and do something about it, to win you away from her. Isn't that when animal instinct is supposed to kick-in? Defending your territory and all that? But I don't think that was ever going to happen, me trying to win you away from her. After all, how could I?

"Once upon a time I would have; you know that too, don't you? I used to be - what? - unscrupulous, self-centred. Yes, even more than I am today! I'm sure, if you wanted to, you could go back into my past and dredge up a few people who would be more than happy to testify to my character - or against it, depending on your point of view. I might even be one of them myself. What a turn up *that* would be!

"'Elizabeth passed the chief of the night in her sister's room, and in the morning had the pleasure of being able to send a tolerable answer to the enquiries which she very early received from Mr Bingley...'. That would be nice, wouldn't it? Being able to 'send a tolerable answer'? All we have - now, this morning - is an *in*tolerable answer.

"You know I may not come back after today, so I'm afraid we might never find out what happens to Jane and Bingley, or Elizabeth and Darcy - though I'm pretty sure it will turn out all right in the end! I say that not because I've read the book before (I haven't, as a matter of fact; shock, horror!), but because I've seen it on the telly. That lovely Colin Firth with his wet shirt stuck to his body... Not a state I've ever seen you in, I might add! More's the pity, eh?

"And I may not come back because Sharon may not want me to any more. She might want to take sole possession of you, now we're near the end; she may want you all to herself, mightn't she? Which is fair enough after all; she's the one you chose to marry.

"No, that's not right. I'm sorry. You didn't choose her did you? Not in the sense that it was A or B, Sharon or someone else; Sharon or me, for example. If it had been, would I have made your decision hard! Under those circumstances she would have been right to be worried she might lose you. But those weren't the circumstances, and she had no need to worry - then or now. And it also wasn't a choice for you because you loved her. That doesn't give you any choice at all, does it, 'love'? I mean, look at me sitting here prattling on…

"Why did you never ask - about me and love, I mean? You might have. More than once I expected you to, to be honest. Not because you had any ulterior motive; nor because you wanted to know for yourself, as if you might be harbouring plans of your own. No. But because that's what friends do, isn't it? Especially when they see people they care about sort of floating along. I don't suppose that's the right phrase, 'floating along'. Certainly not one you would have used in any event. What would you have said? Unencumbered? Too cynical. Unattached? Too staid. Unfulfilled? Too preachy - though who knows? Why don't we pretend that you asked, right now? Your last question. Tie-break time.

"What's that? 'What about you and love, Di?' Is that what you said?

"Why, Jack, isn't that just a little bit personal! Okay, I suppose we've known each other for a few years now, and we are friends. What's that? And you've been meaning to ask for a while but never managed to get round to it? Typical man, that. You ask Sharon if that isn't just typically mannish. Ironically so, in fact, when we think about the connotations of being 'mannish'; being cowardly doesn't come to the fore, does it?

"Anyway, you were saying? Ah yes, me and love. Diana, the Huntress. Did you know that Diana was also connected with virginity? Thought that would make you laugh! Anyway, Diana and love. Interesting idea.

"Let's break it down, shall we? See where we get to.

"First basic question: have I ever been in love? Answer: yes - obviously. Though not, I hasten to say, that often. When I was younger (much younger, of course!), every crush felt like love. Or what a teenage girls imagine love is supposed to feel like. Symptoms traditionally centred around dreamy listlessness, an inability to concentrate; instantaneous blushing when the object of our affection appears - and blushing when they don't. I assume none of this comes as news to you, after all isn't it pretty much the same for men? Oh, I know there will be differences, nuances if you like; but underneath, the emotion's the same isn't it?

"So teenage crushes that were masquerading as love when they weren't. And then you get hurt - inevitably. One day it feels a little different - both the crush and then the disappointment in the failure or rejection. There's something more intense and painful. And then, like so many things, it's the retrospect that tells you that it was love. It's the looking back that allows you to recognise it for what it was, to begin to understand the signs, the red flags. You begin to know what to watch out for.

"I was lucky. My first major failure in love came when I was just turned eighteen, in my final 'A' level year. I say lucky, because it hardened me up before I went to University. You see so many kids at University who haven't had that disappointment. They arrive at college doe-eyed and ready to believe they're in love with the first person of the opposite sex who says 'Hello' to them. Or the same sex I guess, if that's what you like. But because I'd been broken in - to use an unfortunate horsey analogy! - I was prepared. I had an edge, an advantage. I wasn't going to fall so easily.

"The first? He was called Don, not that that means anything to you. He was actually my History teacher. I know, I know! It started out as a crush of course, but when it became clear that he might be prepared to reciprocate - well, that's when I lost all sense of reality. Actually it wasn't that he might be prepared to reciprocate, he *did* reciprocate - and how! I'll spare you that lurid details, but let's just say that I didn't leave school a virgin. And I wasn't one when I found out about his young pregnant wife during the last weeks of term either.

"I went away that summer; a few weeks fruit-picking in France. Just to get some sun, to recharge batteries before Uni. There was no love life there - at least not for me. One or two inadequate physical encounters with boys my age who didn't know one end of a... Sorry; inappropriate! Let's just say that by the time I'd started college, Don was out of my system and I'd begun to define my own personal set of rules and terms when it came to 'the affairs of the heart'.

"University, a fertile ground for love? Is that what you said? Should have been, I suppose. Was for many, in an amateurish, fumbling way. I was choosy by then. A small number of us - girls who'd had similar experiences - gravitated together. We knew what was what, had the same philosophy if you like. I know people thought us a little strange or callous. We didn't mean to be. I don't think I was anyway. Was there any love in those three years? A few very brief encounters really. And one I kind of fell into that ran on afterwards for a couple of years. It was what I needed then, I guess. But was it 'love'? Ultimately, no. No, it wasn't.

"And suddenly that's half a lifetime gone. And here we are, twenty or so years later. Who would have thought that I'd be unmarried and childless at forty-five? Okay, that's ingenuous, I know. And inaccurate. *Divorced* and childless at forty-five. Lots of people might have had money on that outcome!

"You never met Craig, did you? Probably just as well. You would have hated him. And if you *had* met him then I would have hated him even more than I do now because of the comparison with you. Oh I loved him right enough; for about ten years. He fitted me like a glove. We wanted the same things, had the same ambitions. The self-centred, hedonistic, adventure-seeking lifestyle we led was perfect for us. Holidays skiing or scuba diving; restaurants, theatres; going racing - horse, car, you name it. Craig loved his fast cars (more than me ultimately). I thought we were living the dream. I thought *I* was living my dream. And I was crazy about him because of that; because he gave me the freedom to be myself. That's how I saw it.

"Of course that wasn't how it was. Hindsight again. I was trying to bring alive the fantasy I thought I should be living. I had an image of me, as if I was were looking in from the outside, and I was trying to make that come true. It was like some twisted fairy tale. And though I thought I loved Craig as Craig, I actually only loved him - or the idea of him - because he gave me the freedom and space to get closer to that image of myself I so wanted to fulfil. Does that make sense?

"I saw through it all - saw through myself, if you like - eventually. Not too late, I won't say that. If we'd had kids (which neither of us wanted, thank God) then *that* would have been too late. But you know that story, don't you; the bones of me and Craig. So even though you asked me about me and love, there isn't much to tell is there? Not much you don't know about.

"Other than you, of course.

"But you know that, right? I mean, this is hardly earth-shattering news, is it? After we first met, I assumed I was on some kind of rebound; it had been only a year or so after Craig. I was rebuilding my life; rebuilding myself. I had - or so I thought - enough scars and bruises, real or imagined, to last a lifetime. I felt that it was time to re-evaluate, if you like. And because you were already married to Sharon, in a way you were an ideal focal point for me; because you were never going to disrupt that journey I was on. Sounds so pompous, doesn't it?! But I'm sure you get the point. I just needed to be able to park that side of my personality while I sorted everything else out. Investing in you - at a practical, if invisible level - allowed me to do just that.

"I never thought it was love. Never intended it to be so. Maybe it just crept up on me, I don't know. Maybe as I got everything else about my life sorted out - a job, a career, a place to live, an image, a new persona - as all that started to come together, you just grew on me I guess. It was nice that you - and others, I suppose - were there to help me on my journey. Do you remember that time I asked you to come and view some flats with me and we had that stupid argument about orange wallpaper! It might even have been that day, that event, when I suddenly realised…

"But this isn't helping, is it? Either of us, really. Well, I don't know if it's helping you because you're being typically man-like and saying sod all. Which is probably just as well.

"I suspect it will help me. Eventually. Not now. Not today sitting here talking like this. Talking about Don and Craig. Thinking about how I was and how I am. It won't help me when I'm walking out into the car park to drive away, not having had the bottle to wait to see Sharon. It won't help me at your funeral, or probably for a little while after that. Or maybe a long while, who can say? But help, it will. At some point I'll be a changed woman - maybe next year or in five years, who knows? I'll have a revised set of priorities, a new set of success criteria. I'll have readjusted what I want from life. Not just love, though that will be there somewhere.

"Strange, isn't it, how for some people love feels as if it diminishes in importance as you go through life - exactly as others grow to realise just how precious and needed it is. Real love. Part of me envies those people who fall into something at twenty-two or twenty-four and that's it, partner for life, all sorted, nothing left to worry about other than the day-to-day of turning it into a practical, working reality. But most of me, I think, sort of rejoices in gradually and painfully finding out what real love is all about - even if we can't have it; even if all we do is spend our time compensating for that loss.

"I'll return to my career reinvigorated at some point soon, and continue the match upwards. I'll probably make it to some C-suite role sooner rather than later; maybe the Board or something. I'll get a better house, a faster car. I'll add another star to the quality of the holidays I take and the hotels I stay in. And I'll date similarly upwardly mobile men who are looking for - I don't know; whatever it is men look for.

"But I won't be looking for love. If it finds me, fair enough, but I'm doubtful. And you know what? That's actually okay. I never thought it would be until now, but it is. Really.

"Does that answer your question? Let me know if not.

"Now, where were we?

"'Elizabeth passed the chief of the night in her sister's room, and in the morning had the pleasure of being able to send a tolerable answer to the enquiries which she very early received from Mr Bingley…'"

City-break

(October 2014)

"Montjuic?"

The young man in front of him turned slightly, partially removing his attention from the Receptionist who had herself turned to delve in a drawer for a map of the city.

"I'm sorry," he smiled at the young man, as if guilty at having spoken. "I couldn't help but overhear. Montjuic. The best way to get up there is the cable car."

"That's what someone told me."

"You can walk up it - though walking down is better, of course!" Encouraged by the young man's laugh, Jack hurried on. "I'd suggest you get the tube to Paral-lel and then the funicular up to the cable car station. Some people go across from the harbour cable car to get to the foot of Montjuic, but that's not so great for getting to the top."

Having retrieved a map, the Receptionist regained the young man's attention long enough to hand it over. He turned back to Jack.

"You know Barcelona then?"

Jack smiled knowing that their mother tongue conferred a kind of bond between them, even if the young man's accent was an Australian one.

"Yes; one of my favourite places in the world. I'm just here for a few days - for a 'top-up', if that makes sense."

"It does," said the other, sliding the map into a side pocket of his pale green rucksack. "I'm still trying to find places to feel that way about."

Jack edged forward and handed his room key to the Receptionist. The young man didn't move.

"Jack," he said, extending his hand.

"Matt," said the other, shaking it.

"Look, I'd be happy to show you the way up to Montjuic if that would help." They had moved together through the foyer and out into another sunny Barcelona morning. For a moment

Jack paused, breathing in the air, the sounds, the feel of the place. "I was planning to go up there myself today anyway, and I'd be happy to go now if you'd like some company."

Matt had the air of a solo traveller; he was certainly not travelling with a female companion. A quick scan of his clothes, his hair, the bruised rucksack and the partially guarded look in his eyes, told Jack as much. He was sure he too had appeared that way once; perhaps the very first time he had visited the city.

Matt hesitated.

"It's fine, if not. I don't mean to intrude. After all, I could be some axe murderer for all you know!"

"That I doubt," said Matt.

Around fifty-five minutes later they were standing in the castle at the top of Montjuic, leaning against a low wall and overlooking the city spread out beneath them. It had been a pleasant journey up, Matt showing the appropriate degree of enthusiasm for the funicular as it rose from the Paral-lel tunnel, and for the cable car ride up the hillside. It was still reasonably quiet and they had managed to secure a gondola to themselves, something which gave Jack the freedom to point out various highlights as they rose: the old fun fair, the Olympic stadium, Barcelonetta. Once at the top, they had headed into the castle, Jack offering to pay.

"Someone once did the the same for me many years ago," he said, "so I'm really just passing on the favour."

Matt accepted, suspecting the story to be untrue, a fable concocted to ease his acceptance of Jack's generosity. As if to even things out, he had bought two bottles of water from the kiosk outside the gates, and they were now both drinking as they admired the view.

"When do you think you'll decide about your job?" Jack asked, his words aimed at his companion but his eyes fixed firmly on the city, attempting to locate the roof of the El Born Centre.

"As soon as I get back," Matt replied. "The real question is when will I get back?"

They both laughed.

Matt was - to use his own words - "taking some time out". Straight out of university he had fallen into a good job with one of the 'Big Five' accountancy firms and had thrown himself into it with gusto. He had, by his own admission, done well; his first promotion had come after just over twelve months. Now another was on the table, but it was dependant on him narrowing his field of specialisation - and returning to Australia.

"How much time do you have?" Jack asked.

"Officially another week or so. They gave me three weeks, which was great - and then hinted that if I needed a little more time they could be 'flexible'."

"That sounds great. They must really rate you."

"I guess. And don't get me wrong, they're a great firm to work for. It's just…"

"You're not sure about going back home?"

Matt laughed.

"That's an interesting notion. I'm not sure I really know where home is. It used to be Australia until about three or four years ago. And I've been in London since then."

"But neither fit the bill?"

"Something like that." Matt paused. "Which is one of the reasons I'm doing this; touring around, looking at places."

"To see if you can find somewhere you'd like to live?"

Jack saw a large cruise liner edging away from the docks below them, about to creep back out into the Mediterranean and resume its journey, its passengers able to tick off another city from their itinerary. He envied them. He had been lucky in terms of the places he had seen, he knew that; but without his consent, a line had now been drawn through his bucket list. He would be ticking off almost nothing new from here on in.

"Myself, I'll probably going on to Italy: Viareggio, somewhere like that," he said to the ship, "and then Sicily, or Malta, or around and into the Adriatic."

"You talk as if you know all these places."

Jack laughed, more to himself than anything.

"I've been lucky," he replied, turning thought into words, "the places I've seen. Which is one reason, I think, that I can relate to what you're going through, the dilemma you face."

"Have you found your ideal place then?"

"I'd have to say 'places' plural, Matt. But yes. Even though I've never lived outside of the UK for very long, I know the places where I could happily place my hat."

"'Place my hat'? What's that?"

"Oh, some rubbish translation of a proverb from somewhere I expect! I take it to mean somewhere you could settle. You know, take your shoes off, put your feet up."

"Like Barcelona?"

"To an extent."

Jack turned and leant the base of his spine against the wall, now looking across the vast expanse of the citadel's flat roof on which they stood. It was almost as if he didn't want the city to hear what he had to say next.

"I love it here - but I'm not sure I could cope with it on a full-time basis. Barcelona demands energy and commitment. I doubt I have the commitment, and I'm certain I don't have the energy any more!"

It was a statement that seemed layered with meaning. Matt let it go for the moment.

"So if not here, where then? Which places could you live in full-time?"

"If I were your age?"

"No; I mean right now, for you, tomorrow if you had to. And you can't choose England."

"Fair enough."

After Barcelona, Jack would be going home - and doing so knowing that he would never come here again. Worse than that, he knew anywhere he mentioned right now - anywhere - would be little more than a word, an abstract name for a place.

He would never again be able to turn those names into sights and sounds and smells. They would never become new experiences; he had to live off the old ones.

"Tuscany, for sure - even though it can get really hot. Lucca, Sienna, and if I wanted to be a bit more remote, a little place called Montecatini Alto. Bruges - but I'd need to ban all the tourists! - Uppsala in Sweden; maybe Ireland, but not Dublin. And almost anywhere in Switzerland, Basel and Lausanne especially."

"You'd need lots of cash for Switzerland," Matt suggested.

"You've been there?"

"A couple of days in Geneva. Enough to know how expensive it is!"

"There's the rub," Jack said with a slight sigh. "Every place has a thing for which you have to compensate. Everywhere has pros and cons. I like Australia actually. I prefer Brisbane to Sydney, but the heat in the summer! Not sure I could take that every year."

Matt nodded but said nothing. Jack could see him drifting back.

"It's all a question of balance," Jack suggested, pulling his new friend back from wherever he was about to mentally head off. "Nowhere's perfect. Great climate versus hurricane season; fantastic architecture versus hoards of tourists; lakes and streams versus mosquitoes! I don't envy you your choice."

"Well right now it's not much of a choice," Matt confessed, "seeing as I've hardly been anywhere yet. Outside of home and London, there's just Geneva, Berlin, Paris and here. That's hardly comprehensive."

Jack stood momentarily to stretch his legs before easing himself back against the wall. Near one of the corner battlements a group of Orientals had appeared and were singularly preoccupied with taking photographs and selfies on their phones.

"You're right - and they're much of a muchness; I mean, large capital-like cities. But I wouldn't worry about it, Matt. I mean, you're still young. That list of yours may seem short, but it'll already be longer than many people your age. And who says you have to choose yet? I don't think anyone can possibly know what they want until they have lived a little - or a lot. Until they've some scars, some disappointments. Until they know what they *don't* want. You need to have something else on the end of the scales."

"That makes sense."

"I'd suggest that the real question for you is how are you going to accumulate all the 'stuff' you need on that other end of the scale, the stuff you are going to balance yourself against. Whether it's Geneva or here or Timbuktu, you'll only know when you can see those places measured against something else. Maybe that answers your Australia question."

"How so?"

"If you go back home, do you know what you'll put on the other end of the scales? Maybe it'll be places in Asia, maybe even places in Australia; Melbourne, Perth, Darwin. Christ, it might not even be places at all! Could be something completely different."

"Such as?"

"I don't know," Jack said, actually knowing full well. "Maybe a person. Or something you find you like doing; painting, gardening, building things. People talk about achieving a sense of balance in their lives, but fail to think about the 'balance' part. They're just making choices in isolation rather than conscious decisions. Does that make sense?"

Matt, his own eyes now following a group of young students as they trailed around after their teacher, glanced at Jack and nodded.

"I'm talking too much," said Jack, lifting his bottle to his lips. "Sorry."

"What about you, Jack?"

"Me?"

"What's on the other end of your scales?"

The laugh, involuntary again, was filled with the years of experience that divided them.

"I guess I've had different things there at different times. I assume that's natural. You know, what you want when you're young, then when you meet someone... Stuff like that. Priorities change. I suspect the only people who never change what they measure themselves against are exceptional."

"In what way, Jack?"

"Oh, I don't know. Artists, maybe. Or scientists. People who are possessed by the pursuit of or desire for one thing. Einstein and knowledge maybe, or James Joyce and whatever it was that drove him on."

"Doubt I could be that single-minded," Matt said.

"Me neither!" Jack's confession came with a laugh. He watched the Orientals disappear down the steps towards the citadel exit, wondering where they were off to next; where in the city, where in Europe.

"So?"

It was Matt's turn to draw him back.

"'So'?"

"Your balance? I'm guessing - no offence - that you're not some kind of maniac genius who's only ever had a single focus in your life."

"No shit, Sherlock!"

They both laughed, Jack's colloquialism taking Matt by surprise.

"I'm guessing it would have been work at one time, and then probably a lady at another time." Jack nodded as he spoke. "But all the travelling you've done; what's that all about? And what about now? Why Barcelona now?"

The change of expression on Jack's face made Matt suddenly fear that he'd unintentionally crossed a line.

"Hey, I'm sorry, Jack. No need to say, really. I didn't mean..."

Jack raised his free hand very slightly; it was a gesture designed to stop the younger man in his tracks and it worked.

"Don't worry. Really. It's fine."

Jack paused, turning back to face the city. Matt had a sense that he was about to address a wider audience than just him.

"Job, yes - once. Probably when I was about your age. And then a lady. Well, a couple of ladies actually. I loved - love - them both, of course; and the first one taught me how I should love the second. For a while it got a bit crowded on the far end of my scales there!" His chuckle was soft, understated, private. "But that's nothing out of the ordinary. As for the travelling - if that's what you meant - well it was sort of peripheral, never something I did for itself really. I used to have to go places with my work; I enjoyed it. Educated me in what the world was, so that when we went on holiday I was able to make intelligent choices, to know what I'd seen and what I wanted to see. On reflection, it was completely brilliant. If I had to give you one piece of advice, Matt, it would be never stop travelling…"

His voice trailed away, as if it were drifting out across the city, dispersing its syllables like a fine rain on all the places he knew. Matt looked out on the metropolis as if he were watching Jack's words fly away, magically drizzling on the unsuspecting buildings.

In the sudden silence, conscious that there was still something unsaid, he turned to look at Jack. There was a tear running down his cheek, solitary; almost as if it were the manifestation of something that was lost.

"Sorry," said Jack, his hand brushing his face roughly as if he were knocking away a spider's web. "And now? You wanted to know about now?"

"I…"

"It's fine, it's fine," Jack said quickly, intercepting what he expected would be an apology or an attempt to change the subject. He didn't need an apology, nor the subject to be changed. He needed to feel the weight of his situation, to understand it, to know what he was facing. And now seemed as good a time as ever.

"There's only one thing on my scales now, Matt, and that - I'm afraid - is death. The old Grim Reaper has knocked everything else off - everyone else off - and is just sitting there grinning. Grinning and waiting. And because he's so heavy, I'm right up in the air like the little kid on the wrong end of a see-saw with the big fat school bully on the other. And there's nothing I can do about it."

He paused, his words now seeming leaden, not like the fine mist that Matt had so recently imagined they might be.

"I don't understand," he said, as uncertain at this moment as he could ever remember feeling.

Jack tried a smile.

"We're all dying, of course. Nothing remarkable there. But it's one of those things where we live our lives always thinking that it only happens to the other guy. Do you know what I mean? You'd never dream of seeing death waiting for you, would you; see him drumming his fingers impatiently on the table top waiting for the clock to stop?" He took a drink from his bottle and stood up, this time turning to face Matt square on. "Two weeks ago I got the diagnosis from the Doctor. He was calm, professional, as gentle as he could be. During an appointment such as that it's funny how you automatically filter out most of the words said. You end up with a sub-set. In my case it was 'advanced', 'terminal'. Oh, and 'sorry' - as if it was his fault. I left the surgery with my world turned upside down, not knowing what to do. How can you?"

He looked away, back towards his beloved city.

"Which is why I'm here. He said I'd have a few good months left before things got bad. Suggested that I make the most of them before things started…well. The treatments - which I'll begin soon enough - will help, but they'll force me to pay a price too. Pros and cons, Matt; just like everything else."

"I'm really sorry," said Matt. "I know that's useless, but I don't know what else to say."

Jack put his hand on the younger man's shoulder and gave it a squeeze.

"Nothing to be sorry about. You see, like you, I'm 'taking some time out'; seeing some old friends - Lucca, Sienna, here - for one last time. It gives you a different perspective, I'll say that! You know, I've never had to say goodbye before. Not really. Of course we all think that we say goodbye all the time, but we don't. Most of the time when we say goodbye there's always the possibility - however remote - of reconnecting. Well there isn't for me, not now. This is me and Barcelona, a parting of the ways; me certain that I'll never be here again, which - let me tell you - is quite something to come to terms with!"

His low-key laugh forced Matt to his feet. He wanted to do something, to display some kind of emotion or understanding that might just help. But having stood up, he found he was paralysed, unable to move; even his voice was struck dumb for a moment.

"But I have to thank you, Matt, for helping."

"Me?"

"I find myself - I confess - having taken advantage of you. I hadn't planned on doing so of course, by there you are."

"How? I don't understand."

"You see, until now, no-one else knew. I haven't told Sharon yet, mainly because I didn't know how to. I've told my inanimate friends, if you like. The main square in Sienna where they run the Palio; the anfiteatro in Lucca. And now here. But you're my first person, and I thank you for that. It's a liberty, I know. And - I'm sorry to say - rather an unfair one and just a little bit cruel on my part. But I hope you won't hold it against me..."

Jack allowed his words to trail away. Matt had a sense that he was suddenly spent, and from somewhere imagined he could hear a rhythmic tapping sound, a sound like fingers rapping on a table top. He turned and scanned the citadel. From nearby there was the odd click of a camera, a stray voice, the sounds of well-heeled shoes on the stone work. A lone gull wheeled over his head, and from out at sea he heard the blast of a ship's horn.

Turning again to face his companion, he found himself already alone, Jack's figure retreating towards the stairs. Matt could have called him back, but he knew Jack needed to be alone now. He knew he would forego the cable car and walk back down into the city, to say goodbye properly to the hill and the old ruined fun fair. As he watched him go, Matt thought about Jack, and about fate; about London and Australia; and about not saying goodbye.

What He Knew

(March 2012)

It wasn't as if he had always wanted to do 'the Bridge Walk'; that was something for tourists and people without any imagination. You didn't get a true sense of a place by standing hundreds of feet above it, stumbling along some narrow walkway whilst being battered by the wind, the tether to a steel cable your only true security. You got to know a place by being *in* it, immersed in it, knowing its people, understanding the culture, the nuances.

Which, in a nutshell had become his problem. He *did* know the city. He knew the bus routes, the cut throughs, the good restaurants and the bad, the places to avoid after dark. He knew the good discos and clubs, the bars where the most beautiful chicks hung out. He knew the best time of day to take the ferry to Manly, where to catch a wave; the beaches the tourists didn't know about. He knew the mountains, the coast roads, the back roads. He knew every blade of grass in his neighbourhood; he knew the neighbours - hell, he'd even slept with one or two of their daughters!

And now he could add 'education' to that inexhaustible list because he'd been all the way through the system and come out the other side. He knew it wasn't a dead-end, not really. He knew the ultimate reward of his studies was to open doors, to reveal the future fanned out in front of him, displaying all her wares and offering him a choice, temping him to take his pick. It was a prospect that should have seen him excited, enthused; he should have been a young man on the cusp of a new adventure. And he was. But the adventure he wanted was not the one presented to him. And why was that?

Because everything he was being nudged towards, presented with, encouraged to try, clumsily and badly seduced by, bribed with, gifted - everything was predicated on him remaining in Sydney. It was an assumption everyone seemed to make, almost as if he had delegated some of his decision-making to them.

"You've got some great possibilities, Matt," his mother had said just a few evenings earlier. "Not everyone gets options at companies like IBM or the Commonwealth Bank."

"Mum, they're not called 'options'."

"Well, whatever they're called, they don't just hand them out to anybody. You do realise that?"

And of course he did. He knew that based on his grades, his academic 'track record', he stood pretty high in the pecking order. One of his friends, Dill, called it 'The Draft': likening getting a job to the way NFL teams in the States chose new players straight out of college.

"Dude, you're first or second round pick!" Dill had said.

But Matt didn't care. He recognised what great opportunities he might have with firms like IBM, and how, if he did well, they could almost literally open up the world to him. The problem was that he didn't want to wait; he didn't want to have to work in an office for two or three years - to 'do the hard yards' - before he could leave Sydney. And he knew he didn't have to. Some of his friends, Dill included, were taking some time out. 'Travelling' was the euphemistic phrase they used. Most were just going to bum around Asia until their money ran out. And what then? Back to Sydney?

Rightly or wrongly, Matt had come to equate leaving Sydney with freedom and so the sequence of events had become of paramount importance. If he followed his mother's plan, it would be job and career first, leave Sydney second. That was perfect for her for all sorts of reasons, but the wrong way round for him. Dill's plan was to leave Sydney first - though in his case there was no second step in the 'travelling' plan. It was a fundamentally knee-jerk rebellion against 'the system' that had become conventional; and if there was one thing Matt wasn't, he wasn't rebellious. At least not in that way. And although he hadn't said as much, Dill didn't think Matt was the 'travelling' type either. If he had, Matt argued to himself, then he would have invited him along to Vietnam or Cambodia or wherever the hell Dill and his 'Dudes' were going.

Leave Sydney first, step one. But for Matt there had to be a solid step two - which was why, after some short interviews at their local offices, he'd already arranged places on three internship assessment centres in London. These were just two weeks away.

He was telling his mother today, as soon as he'd finished 'the Bridge Walk' and picked up his plane ticket.

Part of him had felt the need to say goodbye to Sydney; after all, she'd been good to him. The only question was how? Matt had considered a final round of doing the things he liked best - his favourite bar, disco, beach, park - but that had promised to be too long and drawn out. He'd seen a flyer for 'The Bridge Walk' and he'd thought "Why not?" For many people it was the first thing they did when visiting the city; for him it would be pretty much his last. And he could stand at the apex and try and pick out all his favourite places in one fell swoop. It would be comprehensive.

And it hadn't disappointed. Having reached ground level again and divested himself of his hi-vis, helmet and harness, walking through The Rocks he found himself surprised just how effective it had been, how much he had been able to see. Indeed, at that moment he felt sufficiently impressed to see himself recommending the experience to anyone in London who might ask him what to do in his home town.

"I know it's cheesy, but do 'The Bridge Walk'; you'll get to see so much. And if I were you, do it just before you leave, not when you arrive."

He was convinced that way round was better. The importance of sequence again.

Leaving the travel agency had - not literally - brought him down to earth with a bump. Hands in his fleece pockets as he walked back toward the bus station, he couldn't help but allow his fingers to feel the boundary of the ticket he had just collected; it was as if its edges, hard and defined, had for the first time made what he was about to do real. A one-way ticket to Heathrow, London.

The flight itself would be an adventure, of course. Being naturally frugal - especially having lived with just his mother for the past three years - he had taken pretty much the cheapest option available, a routing that involved three changes of planes and extended what should have been a journey of twenty-four hours to one almost twice as long. He knew he would have to try and sleep on the planes as much as possible, or grab some shut-eye on those hard, plastic airport chairs. But it didn't matter. It didn't matter that he would arrive in London tired, disheveled and - probably - a little pungent; all that mattered was that he was arriving. The address of the hostel he had booked for his first week was laser-etched into his brain.

Having found a seat on the bus to Greenwich, Matt knew he had about thirty minutes before he would walk through the front door of their home; thirty minutes until he needed to break the news to his mother. He had decided not to wait any longer. Now that the die was cast - now that he could *feel* his ticket in his pocket and there was no going back - he had no reason to procrastinate. Doing so would only make it harder, probably on both of them.

And that would have been doubly unfair. His mother would not take his news well, he was convinced of that. Since his Dad had walked out on them, they'd had to knit together as a team, tight and indivisible. Matt liked to think that was more for her sake than his own, but he wasn't entirely stupid. There had been reasons his Dad had left them, some of which, he had to admit, were entirely understandable. His Mum could be domineering; she had a way of wearing you down. He'd watched her gradually emasculate his Dad, driven him to a point where he just gave in. You can, Matt knew, only do that so many times. He knew she was trying it with him over his 'options'. Of course she wanted the best for him, but she must also have considered what the alternatives were - what real options Matt had - and there was no way any of them could have been favourable to her. Perhaps she was a little scared. Perhaps she was living in fear of the very scenario she was just about to face. And Margie knew what Dill was planning.

Perhaps she was afraid that Matt would do something similar, even though she knew he'd never go travelling with Dill.

"He's a pimp," she'd said one day. It was the fiercest criticism she could give someone without swearing. 'Pimp' was her go-to word when she really wanted to berate someone. Usefully it wasn't gender specific. When she'd heard rumours that Matt had been having sex with Casey from next-door-but-one, she'd said "I know that can't be true, Honey, 'cos she's a pimp of the first order." In his room later that day, Matt had smiled to himself; she'd been both wrong and right.

The bus pulled onto the harbour bridge and Matt looked up involuntarily. He couldn't see if there was anyone walking it from this angle, but guessed there might be. Soon they would be through Milson's Point and heading beyond North Sydney towards Crow's Nest. He'd get off by the church and walk down Anglo Lane. Watching the buildings blur past him, Matt smiled. Anglo Lane; that seemed appropriate, considering where he was heading.

For no specific reason, he found himself remembering the first time he'd had a drink with his Dad. Maybe it was the liquor store the bus had just paused outside as it waited for some lights ahead. They'd gone to a football match; all the way out to see Western take on Melbourne. It had been his eighteenth birthday about a month before. As they made their way home, his Dad had dragged him into a bar.

"OK big man," he'd said, smiling, "what'll it be?"

Matt tried to pretend that he knew nothing about beer, even though he'd been secretly drinking on-and-off for a couple of years now at friends' houses or parties. He remembered choosing something he didn't like but that was well advertised on TV. His Dad had laughed and ordered him something else instead; one of Matt's favourites, as it turned out. That had been the only time he could recall when his Dad and he had hung out as 'mates'. It had been a little difficult; awkward and a bit clumsy. But nice enough in a way. Of course, his dad was already on the slide at that point. Two months later he'd be gone.

He tried to imagine how his Mum would be after he'd left. He would stop her coming to the airport; there could be nothing good for either of them in a scene there. He didn't think he would weaken at the last minute, but you just never knew. Best remove that possibility from the equation. She'd be hit hard, that was certain, but Matt was confident she'd cope. She did when his Dad left. And she had enough friends where they lived. Pat, Fliss and Callie on Carlotta, Bridget just round the corner; they all liked Margie. He suspected Bridget would be her rock - certainly if Megs, her daughter, was anything to go by. He'd miss Megs he suspected, even if she had told him to "fuck off" when he tried to undo her bra that time at Dill's sister's party.

He found himself wondering about the girls in London. What were they like? He knew there was a large Aussie community there, so he was confident that he'd find somewhere to fit in. But he was even more interested in things that weren't Australian. It was a cosmopolitan place; maybe he'd find a Spanish girlfriend, or one from the States, or even Peru! Who could tell? That was all part of the adventure; components of the option he *had* chosen.

Someone else rang the bell for his stop, so he stayed sitting until the last minute. Once on the pavement he checked his ticket again - there it was, those sharp corners - and then started down Anglo. It was a little chillier than he remembered, so he zipped up his fleece. It would be summer in the UK, though someone had told him that the weather was shit even then. He'd already packed most of his things - the ones his mother wouldn't have missed - in his large blue rucksack, now hidden under his bed. After today there'd be no reason to keep it there. He could finish his packing in the open. It might help his Mum come to terms with the fact that he was really going. Turning into Carlotta, he pulled his keys from his jeans pocket. The front door would probably be open, but just in case.

After a few yards he could see the tail of his mother's blue Nissan poking out of the driveway. She was home then. He guessed that was a good thing, considering. Walking up the drive, he leant on the front door's handle and pushed. From inside he could hear the radio in the kitchen.

"I'm back!" he shouted.

Promises

(June 1983)

There was no way she could explain Prince Charming to Todd. He had been trying for the last two months to get her to change her mind. He had made promise after promise; promises she knew he could never keep. And in turn, Margie had made concessions and promises too, even knowing coming back to Brisbane every month would soon prove impractical, and that one day she would wake up over seven hundred kilometres away having forgotten what she had seen in him. While he swore undying loyalty on the assumption that doing so meant something to her, her promises were hollow. It wasn't that she didn't love him, it was that she loved the potential of Sydney more.

Ever since her parents had taken her for that one long holiday - the road trip all the way to Melbourne - Margie had wanted to go back. She was now twenty-four and, even though over fifteen years had passed, had never returned. The young girl's fantasy that said all rainbows ended in Sydney harbour was long since dead, but it had been replaced by others: Sydney was the city where the perfect job awaited, where dreams came true, where you could meet Prince Charming.

"Nothing and everything." This had been her answer to Todd's wanting to know what she could do in Sydney that she couldn't do in Brisbane. "I know I could get a decent job here, I know that." It was clear from his reaction to her somewhat cryptic answer that she needed to spell it out. "And I could move out from under Mum's feet and get my own place somewhere..."

"*Our* own place," he suggested hopefully, and not for the first time.

"Our own place," she corrected herself, adding another empty and impossible promise to her list. "And I know that I could carve out a life that would be good enough to lead. Comfortable, you know? Friends, family; trips out..."

She allowed her answer to trail away, not wishing to add anything too material to it, not wanting Todd to see how much she had thought about it and about what she was giving up. Inevitably there would be elements on any list she made that would leap out at him, just like the popular options on a menu; but not everyone wanted to choose from the table d'hôte. 'Comfort', 'family' and 'home' were all things that ticked boxes on Todd's invisible happiness chart. She wasn't being disingenuous when she said those were important to her too, that she wanted them as much as he did. But the critical thing was that she didn't want them now, she didn't want them in Brisbane - and she suspected that she didn't want them with him. Even though she couldn't be definitive about why, she was virtually certain of the latter and moving to Sydney would either prove or disprove it. In her mind it was the only true test she felt she could apply.

She wanted to go à la carte.

"Your mother doesn't want you to go," he said for what seemed like the umpteenth time. It had become a specious argument.

"No-one wants me to go," she had exaggerated, somewhat robustly, "but that doesn't make any difference. *I* want to go."

"And you're the only one that counts?"

Margie had taken Todd to the edge of the same argument before, part of her wanting him to topple over. If they'd had a blazing row, if he were to demonstrate - in almost any way - that he was flawed, that they might be somehow incompatible, then she would have a trump card to play.

"Right now I am," she said, not bothering to take the defiance from her voice.

As usual he said nothing. Margie wasn't sure if it was because he was too passive or too scared. She was actually glad he always retreated at this point. Had he defied her, had he taken the challenge and flared up, there was always the possibility that she would find such a side to him irresistible. If *she* was scared of anything in relation to Todd, perhaps it was that.

Otherwise her position was bullet-proof. She had been arguing the toss for weeks now, starting with her mother, then on through her friends, and down to Todd. Everyone else - except Todd - had given in; most had moved on from grudging acceptance to being genuinely excited for her. Some were even jealous.

"You'll have to tell us how it's going."

"I'd love to do something like that!"

"If you find anything that would be right for me…"

"I'm so sick of this town too."

She wasn't sick of Brisbane, though; that wasn't why she was leaving. She had given up trying to persuade people that even though in many ways she actually liked Brisbane, she was actually running *towards* something; towards a promise, a chance, and that was a different thing entirely.

But no-one knew that she was running to.

It's all too common for people to associate leaving with the desire to put distance between themselves and something ugly in their lives. Margie had tried - successfully, it seemed - to disabuse her friends of any such notion as early as she possibly could. She had consistently and vehemently stuck to the mantra of 'running to' rather than 'running from'. How could they doubt her? And, other than Todd, from what could she possibly need to escape?

Failure to escape implies being caught, and the fact that she so very nearly had been forced her hand.

Like many things it started with a genuine mistake. For a few it might start earlier, just for a dare; to prove something, that you were 'big' or 'brave'.

"Just stand here and keep a look-out."

"Go over to the counter and buy some Pick'n'Mix, but take your time."

"Pretend you're struggling with your money and get the old guy to help you count it out."

Margie had been fourteen and shopping for clothes with friends in TopShop one Saturday afternoon. It had been busy; the girls giddy. They were trying on t-shirts and denim shorts. She had already bought some things from Myers and was hauling a carrier bag around with her. TopShop was their last stop before they split up and headed home. She had tried on three things but refrained from buying any of them. When she was on the bus going home, she decided to check the colour of the skirt she'd bought in Myers, just to see how it looked in daylight. As she opened the carrier she saw one of the items she'd tried on in TopShop. It was just laying there, price tag uppermost.

Her immediate reaction was to blush profusely, and then quickly check her fellow passengers to see if anyone had noticed. The bus was less than half full and no-one was paying her any interest. She returned her gaze to the t-shirt, her hands now refusing to delve into the bag. It must have fallen in when she was preparing to leave the changing room. How had she missed it? It was too late to go back now, and the family were going out for the day on Sunday. Maybe she could pop in there on Monday after school, or the following weekend. If she were to go back on Monday, she'd need to concoct some kind of story for her parents to explain why she had to go into the city centre on a school night.

Back home, she relegated the contraband to the very bottom of her chest of drawers and then showed her mother the Myers' skirt she had bought.

During the following week she lived in dread of coming home from school and finding the police there, ready to take her away. She was a criminal now and would have to face the full force of the law. She imagined defending herself in court, breaking down in tears, being 'led away'.

"Not feeling well?" her mother had asked on Monday evening when she'd hardly touched her supper.

By Wednesday the fear had subsided a little, enough for her to excavate the t-shirt from the bottom drawer and take another look at it. Of the ones she had tried on, this had been her favourite - and the most expensive. She hadn't been able to justify buying it as she'd already spent most of her money. As she looked at it, she began to construct the scenario awaiting her when she took it back.

"But that was last week!"

"You've had it so long we need you to buy it."

"Audrey, call the police."

As far as Margie could see, there didn't seem to be any scenario that, from her perspective, could lead to a satisfactory outcome.

Come the end of Thursday she had decided to keep the t-shirt. It had been an accident, after all. "One of those things". She was innocent really, wasn't she? And as she snipped the labels from the garment to try it on in the privacy of her own bedroom, she consoled herself with "it's not as if I'm going to do it again". Two weeks later she was back in TopShop. She had loitered a little nervously outside, part of her believing that she would be apprehended as soon as she crossed the threshold. Her friends dragged her in and she waited outside the changing rooms as they tried things on again. Penny bought some jeans, Rosie a pair of dungarees.

The following day she dared to go out wearing the contraband t-shirt for the first time and was unable to avoid the little frisson of excitement doing so gave her. She knew it was highly unlikely that she would be stopped in the street or identified as a pilferer; and the t-shirt seemed to give her license to strut a little more than she was used to - even if such posturing were common for girls her age.

"Oh! So you went back and brought that, did you?" asked Penny, recognising the top. It was as close as Margie came to being found out.

After that the following few weeks were back to normal. School dragged on as only school can, while birthdays for friends came and went. Yet all the while something was growing inside Margie, a slight gnawing that she barely recognised, and when she did, found herself unable to give it a name.

That there was a second 'accident' was probably inevitable. This mishap occurred in a branch of Squiggle. She had gone in to buy a pencil case as a birthday present for Rosie and decided to get herself a few things while she was there. She had a soft spot for pens, particularly pens that were neither blue, black or red. Having made her selection she found herself slightly surprised at the bill quoted at the till. It seemed a little light, but she didn't quibble. When she got home she compared the receipt with what she had in her bag only to discover that the person on the till had missed two of her pens and had failed to charge her for them.

This was not, she argued, the result of anything she had done. She had not tried to hide the pens. It was not her mistake this time, but theirs. She had benefited, yes, and she was in possession of goods that she had not paid for, but again she was the innocent party. What should she have done? What could she do now? This time she had no compunction in keeping the extra items; indeed, she went as far as to assume the purple and orange pens - two of her favourite colours - were the ones she had so fortuitously acquired.

Would it have been possible to put an exact moment on the time and place when Margie decided to experiment? Perhaps when it dawned on her how easy it had been for her to remove those pens, the t-shirt, from their respective stores without anyone being aware? And how much did her family's social standing have to do with her decision, the fact that they were not as well-off as the Rayners or the Pauls? Somewhere in her mind she formed a vague and indecipherable equation that had misfortune, justice, ease, risk, gain and - perversely - inequality as arguments within it. However it might be articulated, Margie had arrived at a theory that seemed worthy of testing.

She started small scale, usually buying multiples of something and half-trying to conceal one when it came to paying. If all the items were counted, she'd feign girlish surprise, blush and pay for everything; there would be no issue. If not...

It proved painlessly easy. Over a period of sever months she acquired a small number of 'bonus' items. She was slightly surprised that she felt no guilt at her actions. The predominate emotional response was the rush she felt on leaving the store, and then the sense of victory perhaps a minute or two later when she was away and in the clear.

From there, the next step - deliberate concealment - was a logical and surprisingly easy one to take. Using the original TopShop experience as a model - buying something whilst deliberately taking something else with no intention of paying for it - worked particularly well with clothes. Take five things into the changing room; choose one to buy; return three to the assistant; secrete one in a bag. Over the next few months Margie's wardrobe expanded much more quickly than her pocket money and the little she earned in the convenience store would allow. Her mother questioned her once or twice over a recent acquisition. "It was in a sale," she would say, or "Rosie gave it to me."

Her mother accepted what she said at face value, and as her escapades in the shops had been so spectacularly uneventful, it seemed to Margie that no-one cared about anything very much - except themselves, probably. Given her mother had been having a difficult time of things recently - her sister, and Margie's aunt, had died, and then she had struggled with various minor illnesses - Margie knew that as long as she was not in any trouble she would be fine. She hadn't considered the consequences on her mother nor her relatively anonymous father. But if she *had* been caught, however...

It was her most audacious undertaking - just two days after her twenty-fourth birthday - that led her to announce to Todd her plan to leave Brisbane.

Nearly ten years of very occasional stealing, undertaken on little more than a whim or as a result of boredom, had become something of a drug to her; an illegal high that avoided the kind of risks she knew Penny had taken from time-to-time with pills from dubious sources - and which had once seen her hospitalised. Compared to that, she had argued what she was doing meant nothing. She was accomplished, a slick operator, and - she told herself - in no way addicted. The idea of moving to Sydney had been growing since she left school but she hadn't yet found sufficient motivation to initiate the process.

She had always steered clear of David Jones as a target for her pilfering. She wasn't entirely sure why. It was probably because she like shopping there too much; ripping a place off tended to mean she stayed clear of it for a while, just in case. It may also have been because she suspected their security was just that little bit tighter. Later, as she sat on the beach at Bondi or walked through the streets of North Sydney, she was still unable to articulate what had possessed her that particular Saturday afternoon.

Her trying-on-clothes-routine had developed to include a variation where you did not try and smuggle goods out in a bag, but actually wore them out of the shop. For that you needed to be wearing either a baggy jumper or a long loose skirt. She'd entered David Jones wearing both. Browsing for a while she chose three t-shirts, a skinny sleeveless jumper and two mini-skirts to try on. As she entered the changing rooms the assistant gave her six tokens, one for each item. Margie tried on all six, primarily to decide which of the t-shirts and skirts she preferred. She dressed, leaving the chosen mini on underneath her original skirt, the t-shirt and sleeveless jumper beneath her baggy top. Then she waited. She had chosen a booth where, if she left a small gap in the curtain, she could see the member of staff on changing room duty.

As soon as the assistant at the desk was different to the one who had served her, she walked out carrying the two discarded t-shirts and the remaining mini and just three of the tokens; the other three she had kicked under a chair in her booth.

"Just too small," she said to the assistant with a smile as she handed the clothes and tokens over.

Walking casually towards the exit, she noticed the original assistant out of the corner of her eye, heading back towards the changing rooms. Margie increased her pace. If she turned right outside the store she would be in the heart of Queens Plaza and, by taking the Queen Street exit, there would be any number of shops in which she could lose herself. A noise from somewhere behind her forced her into a quick change of plan. The Adelaide Street exits were closer. She turned left and headed for those. Another shout behind her, but still she didn't look round. With Kikki.K immediately to her left now, she headed inside as calmly as she could, trying her best to make her way through the store to its Adelaide Street exit as casually as possible. It took her just a few seconds. Still she hadn't dared turn around. Emerging onto Adelaide Street, she found a bus stop just to her left. There was a bus there, doors open, the last person in the queue stepping on board. She ran for it and made it just as the doors were about to close. It was a 175, a bus she knew Penny used.

"Garden City," she said to the driver, pulling out her purse.

As she made her way to a seat, the doors closed and the bus pulled away. She looked back for the first time. The assistant who had served her and a uniformed security guard were standing on the pavement looking her way.

"So what are you scared of?" Todd had asked again one day. She was only three days from leaving. He had tried every other tack for the last few weeks and instinctively wanted one final push. It was a desperate attempt to disprove Margie's 'running from' versus 'running to' argument.

"'Scared'? Why should I be scared of anything?"

"I don't know. Is there something you're worried might happen here, in the future? Is that why you're going away? Because - " he hesitated, "because if it's to do with me, I can change."

Margie knew that Todd had nowhere else to go now. He had never openly admitted that he might be the problem, had never offered to subjugate himself in this way. The fact that he was prepared to go this far was a victory of sorts. It was also the first time he had managed to get anywhere near the truth - the complete truth - as to why she was leaving. Running to *and* running from; that was the nub of it. All she had to do was keep her nerve.

She thought back to the episode in David Jones and how she had acted when she left the store. "Keep calm," she told herself, "don't look back."

"It's not you, Todd," she said, putting her hand on his. He couldn't help but look away. "I keep telling you that. I just need to get away, to try something new, to see what the world - Sydney - has to offer. I'd never forgive myself if I didn't. You know that."

She had one foot on the steps of the aircraft.

The Boardroom Table

(November 1996)

They had obviously spent a significant sum on the new boardroom table. The old one had been showing its age, small fragments of the mahogany veneer peeling at each of its corners. The fact it lacked any in-built network connectivity points and failed to provide access to mains power usually meant that any well-attended meeting would see a mass of cables spreading over the table, often with leads trailing to and from multi-way power bars and network hubs creating trip hazards across the floor. During one meeting - they were about fifteen minutes into the session - Ralph had stood up and suddenly said "Look at this fucking mess!" indicating the plethora of black cables. "And we call ourselves a professional company! When we meet next month this table will be firewood!"

Todd remembered the meeting well, partly because of the expletive his new boss had used. Ralph, a Brit, had been in the business just a couple of months and was finding his feet, but as the new Managing Director he was keen to make an impact and be seen as dynamic, decisive. The table was an easy win; he'd just ask someone to get it sorted and then take the credit. People would confer, murmur approvingly that "Ralph got things done", then point to the evidence.

Sure enough the following month they arrived for their meeting to find a sleek, slightly ovoid table dominating the room. It was the colour of light birch and could seat sixteen easily, maybe twenty at a push. Along its centre, protected by retractable colour-coordinated flaps, five sections each housed four power sockets and four data points, along with a connection for the new projector that had been inserted into the ceiling. "That's what I'm talking about!" Ralph had said in a bizarrely enthusiastic way. Once they had all settled down and the meeting was underway, Todd thought there were probably still as many cables trailing across the tabletop as previously, but had to admit that the new arrangement was far more convenient - and at least the floor-level trip hazards had been eliminated. He wondered if the old table had indeed become firewood, but rather suspected it would have been sold on 'eBay' or handed down to one of their sister businesses. One thing Ralph had made very clear during those first meetings was that they should be under no illusion about the unofficial hierarchy that existed in their Group - and that he was determined their position in it would be secured by promotion to 'the Premier League'. It became evident early on that Ralph liked sporting metaphors.

What was also clear - all too readily and painfully - was that Ralph's man management style left a great deal to be desired. In many ways his approach to the boardroom table was a microcosm of how he treated people. Ralph's predecessor, Craig, had been a calm softly spoken figure from Melbourne who relied on collaboration and consensus to get things done. He listened as much as he spoke, and Todd responded well to such an approach; the growth in his overall standing with his colleagues had been largely down to the way Craig had managed him.

However, from Ralph's perspective people weren't that different to pieces of furniture. If someone wasn't up to the job or might compromise his 'premier league status', he was perfectly happy to move them on. He called it "changing the team", "transferring people in", "getting someone off the bench". During the first few months it proved an approach which had won Ralph a degree of approval as he'd tackled head-on a couple of under-performers, people who had needed to be replaced for some while but who had remained in situ because Craig had lacked the mean streak required to deal with them. Some said he was too soft, too willing to believe in the best of people. Ralph said he was weak - "Within these four walls, of course!"

Although he was instinctively cautious as far as Ralph went, initially Todd was prepared to cut him some slack; he had, after all, improved the team through his 'transfer policy', and the numbers at the end of his first quarter had suddenly jumped back into positive territory. That was good for all of them. Todd had hoped that having deliberately set out to make waves and shake things up, Ralph would then settle down and take a more measured approach - one more akin to Craig's.

It proved to be a wish that was to remain unsatisfied. Once Ralph had got the ball rolling, once he had "pulled them back from the brink of defeat", he upped the ante even more, became even more authoritarian. Those who responded well to such a brutal style - Chris from Operations and Declan from Manufacturing in particular - lapped it up. In Todd's eyes they became fawning acolytes, and the more they fawned the more Ralph leant on them.

Todd began to see the cracks appearing after around six months. Chris and Declan were working sixty hour weeks. In order to get through their work, they had become reclusive and incommunicative; and more or less everyone else on the team was trying to up their game to stay in Ralph's good books. Some of his colleagues - excluding Chris and Declan - began to talk about the two Execs Ralph had let go, deciding that "they weren't so bad after all", and in after-work drinking sessions Craig was more than once posthumously heralded as the embodiment of a model manager.

In many respects Todd was lucky. He had found a niche for himself in Research & Development and, under Craig's guidance, been promoted to head of function. Theirs was a complex and somewhat protected department; everyone knew that's where the real brains of the company lay, and that they needed to be left alone "to do their thing". Break R&D and the business would suffer. Because of this - and because Ralph didn't really understand R&D - most of the time he left Todd to manage himself and his people. Occasionally there would be the odd explosion, a rocket sent in his direction, but he - along with Laura, the HR Manager - were on relatively safe ground.

Dela wasn't so lucky. She had been parachuted in to run the Finance function some nine months previously, taking interim control until the incumbent returned from a prolonged period of medical leave. When they didn't come back, Craig gave her the job full-time. Everyone knew she was out of her depth, but she got by thanks to Craig's patience and the solid support and understanding of her colleagues. One or two - and Declan in particular who had never warmed to Dela - had openly speculated whether she might be next for Ralph's chop. However, given Ralph was focussed elsewhere in the first few months - and then busy basking in the glory of seeing the numbers turn - it appeared she might survive. Todd hoped so. He liked Dela; she was one of the more sociable types - and one who actually made a real effort to try and understand what he and his team did.

It was Declan who "started the ball rolling", the phrase coming to him as being redolent of one of Ralph's clichés. Partly due to his enormous workload and partly out of something akin to spite, Declan reduced his support for Dela, choosing to be slightly less helpful with production of the month-end figures than she needed him to be. It only took a moment to sew the seed.

"Do you have the report for Declan's area?" Ralph had asked. It had been a routine question, asked in an open forum.

She had pushed some papers towards him.

"Output up just under two percent; margin impact neutral."

"Interesting," Ralph had said fingering the sheets somewhat vaguely. Todd saw the warning signs immediately. "Declan's own numbers - which I've gone through with him thoroughly - suggest nearly three percent and a one percent margin benefit."

He let the statement hang there, teetering on the verge of being a question but not quite toppling over.

"Really?" Dela shot Declan a look that blended confusion with animosity. "I'll take another look, of course. Declan, if you can show me where you got your numbers from…"

Declan nodded graciously and passed her a pack similar to the one he had previously given Ralph. Todd could see he had come prepared.

Dela entered the next monthly session a few minutes late, slightly flustered. Todd noted how Declan and Chris exchanged glances then looked towards Ralph, the three of them sitting as a little triumvirate at the top of the table. He knew what was coming; he had seen it before, in those early days. He now knew how Ralph operated and could tell his mind was already made up.

The meeting followed its usual pattern; each of Ralph's direct reports would give their update for the month, presenting achievements, progress and issues to the team. His own slot passed with little incident. His team was working on the final details for a new product, and Ralph emphasised how important this was to all of them, and how, in two months' time, he was expecting a full briefing for the team. Todd would be front-and-centre then.

When it came to her turn, Dela plugged her laptop into the projector and started walking them through the headline numbers for the business unit. Todd noticed Ralph almost immediately engaged in sidebar conversations with Declan and Chris. Their rudeness annoyed Todd; it appeared Ralph wasn't listening or concerned.

"Can you just go back," Ralph suddenly said as Dela skipped on a slide, abruptly demonstrating that he had indeed been paying attention. It was an ability that alarmed them all. "That number there; the 4.2 percent. Is that correct?"

"I'm sorry," Dela was slightly taken aback, "what do you mean?"

"I mean, is it correct? You're sure it's 4.2 and not 4.1 or 4.4?"

"We ran all the standard reports from the system, just as we always do, then checked the output twice. I don't understand why it wouldn't be correct."

Ralph looked at Chris who, saying nothing, just shrugged his shoulders. There was a short and uncomfortable pause and then Dela pressed on, clearly rattled. Two slides later, Ralph stopped her again.

"Why isn't the bad debtors' figure going down? We all agreed that it should."

"It *is* going down, Ralph," Dela was clearly on the defensive. "It's down two percent on last month. I can show you the figures…"

"Two percent!" He laughed. "That's no bloody use is it? Two percent."

All eyes were focussed on him, but when it was obvious that he was going to say nothing more, everyone looked back towards Dela. It was instinctive. The team felt for her - some more than others - and it was clear she was in his cross-hairs. She made some remark about revalidating the numbers, and then pushed on. Ralph disengaged, and for the remainder of her session was talking almost incessantly with Declan.

"That went well," she said to Todd as they left the boardroom.

"It was just your turn," Todd suggested. "Maybe it will be me next month."

But it wasn't. It was Dela's turn again. This time Ralph paid almost no attention to what she was saying from the moment she started her slot. When it came to the bad debtors' number, Todd felt Dela hesitate before she reconfirmed the previous month's data and then reported a further three percent reduction.

"We'll never get there at this fucking rate," Ralph said to Chris, but loud enough so that everyone could hear.

"That's not fair, Ralph."

Todd's words had escaped before he could do anything about them. All eyes turned his way.

"What?" said Ralph.

One of Ralph's favourite phrases - 'there's blood in the water' - was suddenly front-and-centre in Todd's mind. It might not be just Dela's blood now. He had to respond.

"I don't think what you said is fair. We've all got a hand in the bad debtor's number. I know it's Dela's department who have the responsibility, but she needs others" - Todd looked at Declan with meaning - "who have a part to play."

"Well, Todd, let me tell you this. I think what I said *is* fair. You're right, it's Dela's 'R', and clearly the numbers are not good enough, are they?"

"Maybe they're not what we targeted..."

"I rest my case!" interjected Ralph triumphantly.

"…but there's no need to be rude about it."

"Rude?!"

In spite of himself, Todd felt the water becoming saturated.

"You and Declan have been talking through Dela's whole presentation. She's tried to explain the numbers. I think the rest of us are on-board."

Todd let the words drift across the table, glancing around in the hope that someone would back him up. Settling on Dela last, he could see at least she was grateful for his intervention.

"Well, well," said Ralph, stepping into the centre of the silence. "I'm being rude am I? Well I'm very fucking sorry, Todd. But from where I'm sitting the numbers aren't under control, and they're not coming down as fast as they should. And it's my fucking arse on the line when I have to present these to Greg and the Exec Board. Comprendi?"

"Of course…"

"And on that basis, it's my job to do something about it, isn't it? And how I choose to do that is down to me - or do you have a different view you'd like to share with us?"

Once again they were all looking at Todd. Declan, smiling, whispered a comment to Chris loud enough to ensure Ralph also heard it. Ralph smiled

"Well?"

"Of course, but there's no need to be such a bully about it…"

There were one or two gasps which escaped at that point, most noticeably from Laura who - like the rest of them - had been keeping their heads down. Ralph, whose face had reddened perceptibly, looked her way. There was a challenge in his eyes that seemed to say "if you're going to say something, you'd better say it now." She remained silent.

"Well," Ralph said, his voice trembling as he tried to keep it under control. "Now I'm a bully, am I? That's not company policy, is it Laura?" She remained silent, as he had known she would. "Dear, dear. Who else agrees with our friend from R&D?" Silence. He paused for effect. "I'm afraid you've just crossed a line, Todd. I've known all along what you think about me, so I'm not surprised at your outburst. And I'm almost impressed that you should choose to do so in defence of a colleague considering it wasn't even your turn." Ralph looked around the table, letting everyone know that their time would come. "But let's make it your turn, shall we? Yours and Dela's. Right now. You've done me a favour; saved me some time. 'Kill two birds with one stone'. Chris, get the IT guys to rescind Dela and Todd's systems' access immediately; email, everything. You two, leave your stuff here and get out. You're fired, both of you; incompetence and insubordination. Laura will be in touch, won't you Laura?"

Neither Dela nor Todd moved. No-one spoke.

"Well? Go on, get out. Out. Straight out. Get your coats and bags or whatever, and just get the fuck out of here. Go!"

Apart from Ralph, Declan and Chris, everyone else looked down as Dela and Todd walked to the door, opened it, and left. All they could focus on was the nearly-new birch table.

Walkabout

(November 2013)

"Hello Edward.

"It's funny. I've always found your name so formal, ever since we were young - and now here I am wondering why we never managed to shorten it. Perhaps neither of us are the type. Or maybe we left it too late, so inculcated by our parents into the formality of 'Ralph' and 'Edward' that by the time we were old enough - and free enough - to do as we pleased the opportunity was gone. Old habits and all that.

"I can't say it's ever bothered me to be honest. It's only now, writing this that I think of it again. Unlike you, I've spent my whole life trying to live up to my name; to see if I could suit it, fill its boots, be worthy somehow. Not that I ever liked it. I always preferred your name, but it's not the sort of thing you can swap is it - not that you would have wanted to.

"I'm carrying on writing in the hope - which may be forlorn, of course - that you're actually still reading this. That, after all this time, I still 'count' one way or another. How long has it been? Sorry, rhetorical question given we both know <u>exactly</u> how long it's been. 21st June 1993. Just over twenty years. Twenty years since you married Catherine. Twenty years of not forgiving you for stealing her away from me. That's a long time to bear a grudge, isn't it? A long time to remain silent. At least you'll have some idea by now how pissed I was with you.

"I can't remember how I heard, but I did hear about Catherine. I'm sorry. You must miss her terribly; I know I did. Don't worry, the first fifteen years are the hardest, not that you'll probably live that long, eh?

"Sorry, a little cheap and below the belt. But perhaps that's how you'll remember me? I doubt you'd recognise the Ralph who's writing this now, lying between these stiff starched sheets, black Mont Blanc in hand. Tool of the trade in one sense only, I'm afraid.

"Anyway, I won't have to worry about remembering things much longer, having been told that I 'need to get my affairs in order'. I think that's the time-honoured phrase isn't it? And there <u>you</u> are, one of my 'affairs'; and this little missive is the attempt to 'get you in order'. Makes it sound as if I'm trying to tidy you away, put you back in your box - when in actual fact it's probably more likely to be the other way around. Am I a loose end for you, Edward? Perhaps you don't think of me at all, I don't know. Perhaps this letter will result in the opening rather than the closing of a box. A little trinket box. Or Pandora's box.

"In many respects this letter isn't about you at all. How can it be? What can I say about someone I haven't spoken to for so long? I've had snippets from others as to what you've been up to, but not so much since Renee died. For a short while Catherine used to send me a Christmas card each year with a little letter inside it; did you know that? So for a time I'd get an annual update on your rise to corporate stardom - something I desperately tried to emulate and spectacularly failed at. But more on that later! I don't know if Catherine expected me to write back. When I moved here in ninety-nine I gave very few people a forwarding address, so for all I know there could be a sad little pile of unopened Christmas cards sitting in a Post Office depot somewhere... Having said that, other than the usual stuff about kids growing up, I doubt there'd be much in there that would surprise me - after all, you aren't an exciting individual are you? If you'd changed your ways and become a bullion thief I think I might have heard of it!

"So let's pretend, shall we? Let's pretend that you do care a little bit about your long-lost brother, the black sheep of the family. Let's pretend that, in order to make some kind of peace - on both sides, who knows? - you need to be 'filled in' on the last few years of my life. Affairs in order, and all that. And, hey, it might prove therapeutic for me too - though considering the state I'm in, I can't say I really give a stuff any more. Which might be par for the recent course if you were to ask my friends - if I had any friends to ask that is.

"Shall I scene set? I'm lying in a hospital bed, private room, pretty nurses, (all that money leaking into insurance policies finally paying off) waiting to die. All things considered, I'm feeling surprisingly okay. They say I have a few weeks to live at most, though you wouldn't know it from the way I can still carry on sometimes! I reckon it'll be less than a month. As soon as they can't respond to my demands, can't keep stepping up the drugs to keep me lucid then I reckon I'll slide quickly. I think I want to. In spite of all circumstantial evidence to the contrary I was never much of a fighter. I won't tell you exactly where I am because I don't want any ill advised flights on your part seeking a 'last minute reconciliation'. Not interested. Which is why I'm having someone post this from Dubai during a stop-over on their way back to the UK. Could be almost anywhere east of there, see?

"I'm assuming that you're probably au fait with the following couple of years after I failed to show for your wedding - though I also suspect you'd stopped caring about me before the end of that fateful day. And you had other fish to fry, didn't you? Would you believe that I was actually dressed and ready to go to the wedding? Then I stood in front of the mirror and just couldn't go through with it. Thank God you hadn't asked me to be Best Man! It had been hard enough swallowing my pride the previous two years, but the thought of turning up and playing the role of the loving brother, blessing your marriage with Catherine... That would have been a step too far.

"It's funny, I went back to work the next week somehow inspired. I'd never been that bothered about what I did for a living, to be honest; nor how I did it. We were like chalk and cheese there. You were so professional, successful, ruthless even. Stealing Catherine must have felt like taking candy from a baby brother, eh? And it worked for you, Edward, didn't it? And because you were intelligent and had that detachment about you, it was easy. I didn't have the gumption to act the way you did, but I did decide it was my turn to be successful. Whatever it took. Perhaps there was part of me that imagined I might even win Catherine back from you.

"I was a street-fighter compared to your smooth elegance; you would jab and move while I just slugged it out. But sometimes it works out for sluggers. Just then our company needed people like me. They didn't care how we got results, just as long as we did. I found I had a talent for it, you might say. I was promoted a couple of years later, made MD of my own part of the firm. Brisbane of all places. Told to go and turn the business around. Which is what I did. 'Take no prisoners' they said, so I didn't. Was it pleasant? Not especially. Did I enjoy it? I guess part of me did. Eighteen months later we were the fastest growing part of the company. I wasn't popular, made a number of enemies I guess, built up a reputation; but all means to an end.

"A year later, they offered me the whole of Australia and New Zealand. They said it had potential but was under-performing. Would I sort it out? I wasn't going to say 'no' was I? And you know what I found? It was easier. My reputation touched down before I did. People started pulling their socks up before I even walked through the door; because they knew what a bastard I could be, most of the time that was enough. It was as if I had a small thermonuclear device in my pocket that I could set off any time I wanted to. After three years we were pulling double digit growth, doing stupid margins. Even you, my clever brother, would have been proud of me. Maybe.

"I remember taking a long holiday then. Must have been 2001 or so. I hired one of those big RVs and just headed out of Sydney; decided I'd drive for a couple of weeks and then find an airport and fly back. It was like one of those 'finding yourself' trips you'd banged on to me about just after you'd stolen Catherine. Having taking my reason for being away from me, you had the nerve to suggest I needed to go and find it. But I had already found it, you stupid twat!

"Sorry. Uncalled for... Maybe I should cross that out?

"There hadn't been anyone since Catherine; no-one important, anyway. Having been successful - after a fashion, at least - I wondered what was missing from my life. I was at least self-aware enough to know that there was a hole I'd never been able to fill since Catherine left me. I even wondered if there was a hole there because I'd left you - if you see what I mean. I remember sitting in the outback one evening, a day or so out from Ayers', drinking beer, watching the sun go down, and wondering if it wasn't time to bury the hatchet. I actually thought about calling you. I was looking in that bloody mirror again - though this time not quite so dressed up! And you know what? Same answer… Fuck him.

"Had I answered any 'big' questions on my road trip then? Did I return to Sydney an enlightened/changed/better man? (delete as appropriate). I doubt it. I sort of drifted for a short while, a little bored. Goal achieved in Australia, I was beginning to get itchy feet. Then out of nowhere an offer to take over the Asia-Pac region for one of our main rivals. They wanted me based out of either Singapore or Hong Kong - my choice - and to be responsible for everything between the Suez canal and the west coast of America. That was like half a planet! Of course I said yes. But you know what else I said? Before I signed on the dotted line, I asked them what kind of a leader they wanted me to be. I think they were a bit confused by that. I had to spell it out for them. I told them about the 'win-at-all-costs' version of me, and the 'only-be-nasty-when-you-really-needed-to-be' version. 'Culture fit' they said. Whatever. I assume they'd done their homework, so they shouldn't have been surprised by my asking.

"There was actually a third option; the one I didn't give them. The 'be-like-Edward' option. Funny that. And it turned out that's the me they wanted; a me I hadn't even invented yet. They'd seen the results - my results - and that's what they wanted, but they wanted the results their way. I could have turned it down. Maybe I should have turned it down… If I'd asked you - if we'd still been on terms, as it were - I'm pretty sure you'd have just laughed in my face. 'No chance', you'd have said. And guess what? Bingo! Right again, big brother.

"But I thought 'what's the big deal?'. I mean, how hard can it be, right? But it was; it was tough. I saw quickly enough what needed to be done, and if I'd been my old 'slugger' self I would have been able to cut through the crap pretty quickly. But I couldn't. I was forced to be nice, dance round the handbags, not upset anyone. Things improved, but only very slowly. It was agony. It took all my willpower to avoid flying off the handle - with everyone. Instead of coming out of my shell in order to be Mr. Nice-Guy, I retreated into it. I couldn't be what they wanted me to be. I couldn't be you. I confess I got pretty low for a while; my social life - what little there was of it - went to Hell in the proverbial hand-cart.

"I was beginning to feel like a failure. And what was worse, I think I was beginning to look like a failure. And then I had my brilliant idea. I knew what needed to be done - especially on the commercial side - and I knew how to do it. As I was struggling to get my guys to understand, I thought I should do one or two deals myself, in the background, just to nudge things along. Seemed to make perfect sense. So I created a 'profile' for myself and started to be a little more 'operational'.

"Small scale to begin with; the odd punt here and there. Some of them were a little risky, but paid off. When people asked me about this new guy who was making these nuggets of contribution, I said he was someone I'd known from way back who I'd contracted to help us out. It was a little irregular, but not illegal so they didn't stop me. Funny, isn't it, that people will pretty much let you do whatever you want as long as they get what <u>they</u> want out of it? Anyhow, the numbers began to edge up. 'Jack' - my nom-de-plume - had one or two reverses, but on average over a rolling month he was maybe averaging somewhere between 50%-100% gain on investments. The rest of the team were struggling to get into double digits!

"I knew all the regular guys wouldn't touch the sorts of deals I was prepared to do; they all had careers and families to think about. I had none of that. No family, and I didn't see myself as a 'career' kind of guy. I started getting a little bolder, taking a few more risks. The swings were wilder, but the returns were still good. It seemed to Head Office as if Asia-Pac was on the rise. Zero to hero. Bingo!"

"Have you ever had that little voice that starts chipping away at you sometimes, telling what you should and shouldn't be doing? You probably have. In the mid-nineties yours would have probably have been saying 'Steal Catherine! Steal Catherine!' Whatever. And I bet you always listen to yours don't you? Gut instinct maybe. Well my little voice started about then. It was telling me to stop. Telling me that I should 'retire' Jack; to get out while I was ahead. But I didn't listen, did I? There was one huge deal - bigger than I should ever attempted - that didn't quite work out. We took a hit; cost us two months' profits. I was called to HQ. They wanted to meet 'Jack'.

"I had two options. I could come clean and probably get the sack, be disgraced. Maybe even jailed. Or I could fall on my sword and hope for the best. I chose the second. I wrote a long apologetic resignation letter, admitting that I had let them down, let the region down; that I had allowed Jack too much free rein. I said that I'd terminated my arrangement with him. I said that, under the circumstances, I felt the only honourable thing to do was to resign with immediate effect. They liked honour. I threw in a line about leaving the region in a better shape than when I'd started. I knew that was true; I knew they had to cut me some slack for that. There was a little to-ing and fro-ing, but in the end they agreed to let me go. I'm pretty sure there were one or two of them who had an idea that if they dug too deep it wouldn't reflect well, so they cut their loses - which was a good deal considering they were ahead! I was on edge for the last few months, expecting at any time to be found out, hauled in, arrested. After the year-end figures were published, I was confident I was in the clear.

"That was ten years ago. I was nearly sixty. Sixty! I'd just torched my career pretty much; I had no family, no roots. I was an old single guy who'd 'done' Singapore for the last few years. Most men in my position would have a professional parachute: back to a role in Europe, a promotion into a desk job States-side. I didn't. My future looked like the Outback. Still, I'd done one shrewd thing at least. For every ten bucks Jack invested, I added ten cents of my own. Over the year or so he was operating, I'd built up quite a decent nest-egg. I'd avoided the too big or too risky deals - like that last one! - so never made any major loses. Maybe that's how I should have operated for the company. So I was lucky. As long as I didn't go crazy I had enough cash to keep me going for a while - a long while if I was super careful.

"Have you ever not known what you were going to do, Edward? I doubt it somehow. It's a strange feeling; both frightening and liberating. Having decided that it was time for Singapore and I to part company, where next? If we were talking like-for-like, then I didn't fancy Hong Kong; I liked Asia, but not Hong Kong. I could have just gone back to the UK and played the role of the retired ex-pat. I thought about Dublin, or Italy. Loads of places. But every option seemed to involve putting down roots, and though I was clearly old enough - too old, some might say! - that didn't appeal. So I went back to Oz. Stayed in Perth for a while and then did the old RV thing again, though this time from the other side. I had this vague idea about doing it coast-to-coast, but very slowly. Taking years even.

"Sound daft? Probably was. In spite of all I'd done, the experiences I'd had, I felt empty. I had this vague notion that I needed to fill myself up somehow, though I had no idea what with. This time the RV trip really was a voyage of discovery, an attempt to try and 'find myself'. Nearly thirty years or so before that I'd had a plan, of course. A conventional plan which involved getting married - did I mention Catherine recently? - settling down, having kids, a decent job. I'd live in a decent place, be a decent bloke; an average, normal, contented bloke. Maybe it had been more than a plan; maybe it had been a dream. But it wasn't a dream any more. I didn't have - hadn't had - a 'dream' for quite a while.

"You must have retired by now Edward. Maybe eight or nine years ago? Retired to your conventional retirement - though Catherine's dying would have probably screwed that up well and truly. Still, I daresay you've managed. Kids rallying round; grand-kids too, probably. Pillar of the community? On the parish council, maybe. Or the local council. Running as an MP even, who knows. You will have coped, Edward. You always did. When were you ever unable to cope? I never saw it.

"Anyhow, I bought this nice RV - comfortable enough to live in for a while - and headed out of Perth. I'd kicked my heels around there for a while and then one day knew it was time to move on. I headed north. You'd be surprised, but there are lots of national parks in Australia. I'd had enough of city life for a while, so decided to navigate via these. That's where I'd park up and stay, to be on my own, to see if I could like myself again. Because I realised I didn't. I don't know when I'd lost that self-respect. I think I confused it with self-esteem, and when I was the bully-boy I lived off that, off my results. Tangible stuff feeds self-esteem. But I'd discovered that self-respect was a whole different ball-game.

"I took my time. I went north - slowly. I experimented. I'd taken along a camera, books, pens, paints, paper, all sorts. I tried carving bits of driftwood I'd found on the shore and ended up making a fire with the results. I'd download my photos onto the laptop I'd taken with me (I'd actually taken two!), but they were just useless tourist shots no matter how hard I tried to be creative or 'arty'. Briefly I tried to draw and paint, but ended up with crap that not even a five-year-old would be proud of! See how hard I tried, Edward, on this voyage of discovery?

"When I reached Shark Bay - maybe after a week or two - I tried to write to you. I thought it was worth a shot. But I couldn't get started, not really. The letter was nothing like this; it was how I imagined a letter should be, not how it needed to be. I threw the beginnings of three attempts away, in the fire along with my driftwood sculptures! But I'd enjoyed the process. So I tried writing a letter to Catherine. Of course, there was no way she was going to read it, but I thought I'd try to exorcise my ghosts. Why not? It wasn't great, and never quite what I wanted to say either, but at least I finished it. And I didn't burn that one until much later.

"The thing that amazed me the most was that I actually enjoyed the process of writing. One day I sat by the shore, notebook in hand, and just wrote about what I could see. I had no idea what I was doing really, but I'd found something that absorbed me, and maybe that's what I needed above all else; a process. I'd been semi-successful at work when I was playing a role, in the part, the process of being the boss. I wondered if it wasn't the work, the results or how I went about it that was the big hook, but the fact that I was operating a machine, my machine. I didn't have enough talent for whittling or painting to take me out of myself; my lack of ability always got in the way. But with writing, well, it was something I could manage adequately - which meant I could absorb myself in it. Does that make sense? (And now I'm practiced, it means I can actually write and finish a letter to you.)

"I stayed at Shark Bay a couple of months, maybe twelve weeks. There was a supermarket, a gas station, a camp where I could park up in safety. I could live cheaply. I swam a little, took a boat out occasionally. I even talked to people! But mostly I would write. I got into a little routine. Was I happy? Probably not, but it was as close as I'd come for a long while. I could sense my self-respect rousing from its slumbers. I actually started to like this new guy a little bit! I'm sure lots of people I'd worked with over the years wouldn't have been able to recognise him, but hey ho.

"During my second month there I wrote something about Shark Bay, what it was like from an outsider's perspective. Not a day tripper, but someone who was more immersed in the place. I told someone at the gas station about it and they persuaded me to send it in to the letters page of the 'Geraldton Guardian'. I couldn't see the point to be honest. But then they published it, and not as a letter either. Called me a 'Guest Correspondent'; got a few column inches. I was stunned. And the most remarkable thing was that something I'd done for myself had value for others. I was used to things working the other way round.

"Anyway it established a pattern. I eventually moved on and tried the same formulae, staying for a while in a place to get to know it, then write about it. Most times I didn't bother sharing what I'd written, sometimes I did. I'd usually get published in the local press if so; they were so desperate for material I suppose. Coral Bay, Exmouth, Dampier. I'd mainly stick to the coast, though I'd go inland for time-to-time; the Kennedy Range, for example. Near Dampier there are some islands, West Mid Intercourse Island, East Mid Intercourse Island. How wild is that?! There's a bridge to the East Mid one; I just had to see what went on there...! Nothing, as it turns out. I spent a month or more at Port Hedland. You get the picture. One way or another, it took me half a year to get to Darwin.

"By the time I'd arrived there I'd managed to build up a little portfolio of all these occasional bits and pieces I'd written. A guy I'd met in Dampier told me to look up a friend of his, Bart, someone who worked at the Northern Territory News. I showed him what I'd written. Bart liked it; he also liked the fact that I was a Brit, said it gave a different insight into Australia. He wanted me to write something similar for his paper; wanted to know if I would be prepared to do a series. He even offered to pay me, so I knew he was serious! The money didn't matter as much as the offer. This was about me and what I could do, by myself, for myself. What I could deliver without the machinations of big business.

"I stayed in Darwin for three years. Travelled all over the territory, including three months in Alice Springs, often out and back to Uluru. And you know what, Edward? It was brilliant. I felt as if I'd found something at last. A niche; my niche. The News ran my monthly column for two years. I became something of a minor local celebrity I guess. I wrote under a pen name; don't ask my why, I just did. Maybe I was still afraid that my past would catch up with me one day. So for a while - ever since Shark Bay actually - when I wrote I became Jack Watson. It wasn't that Jack was an alter ego; he wasn't. He was still me. Was then, is now. Jack and I have been inseparable!

"While I was in Darwin I started writing something else too. I'd managed to get this crazy notion in my head that I could be a 'Writer'. Not just some guy who trotted out the odd piece of colour for the local rag, but a proper writer; a writer with a capital 'W'. I'd met this lonely, mixed-up lady when I was in Port Hedland. We used to drink together occasionally. I'd buy her a drink, she'd tell me her life story. It doesn't matter who she is, that's not the point. It was her story that was important. It was interesting, complex; it became more an idea than a story after a while. The kind of idea you can do something with. Consciously or not, I started to play with it, build it out. By the time I'd left Dampier it had started to grow arms and legs. Bart's offer was delivered with impeccable timing; it gave me a reason to settle for a while and to work on this story. Did I know what I was doing? Definitely not, but that didn't stop me. Again it was process; process and purpose. Before I left Darwin I asked Bart if he could recommend someone I might send it to. I didn't think it was really any good mind, but I just wanted to know, to test myself. He gave me a contact in Brisbane; Josh Thompson. I posted the draft the day before I left Darwin along with a message to say that I'd turn up in Brisbane at some point in the next year. When I arrived there maybe six months later, Josh was waiting for me.

"Long story short, he'd liked it. Said it needed some work, rough edges and all that, but if I was able to polish it sufficiently then they'd seriously consider publishing it. No money changed hands, after all I was an unknown Brit with a modest - and short! - track record. Yes, I came recommended, but that wasn't worth much really. It was another deal to keep me located in a place for a while; another process to go through. Six months later the book hit the shops. You won't have heard of it - you certainly wouldn't have been looking out for Jack Watson!

"'Impartial Certainties' did okay, in spite of the title. A minor ripple, you might say. Sold a few thousand, made the old book club list. I had my photo in the paper back in Darwin: '(Not Quite) Local Boy Come Good'. Something like that. Josh was interested in a follow-up; interested but lukewarm, I think. I could have used that as an excuse to stay in Brisbane, maybe even settle there, who knows? But I wasn't sure it was for me; I had history in Brisbane, don't forget. And anyway, I was running out of time on my extended visa, and my RV still needed to clock a few more miles before I sold it on.

"In any event, the major deal-breaker was that I'd got my diagnosis while I was there. An unhappy prognosis, discussions about treatments, quality of life - the usual shit. I won't bore you with the details. On the face of it another reason to remain in Brisbane, you might think. Maybe you'd have been right. But that wasn't where I wanted to end up. God knows, it wasn't <u>how</u> I wanted to end up!

"So I just head out. Spent a few months in NSW, Tasmania, until it was time to head - well, here. Again I thought about going back to the UK. Going 'home'. Except it wasn't home any more. Nowhere was. My RV may have been the closest I came, sad as it may seem. When things got so that I couldn't look after myself any more I pulled out the old insurance policy and the rest, as they say...

"Any questions? There will be a test later...

"'Did I carry on writing?' Nope. Figured I'd proven all I needed to prove to myself. I picked up the camera and had a second run at that. The results were a little better, but by then it didn't really matter did it?

"'Did you meet anyone?' I met loads of people... Oh! you mean 'meet' like that; the inverted commas kind of 'meet'. Not really. Occasionally there were connections; Renee came closest. For a while she became my link to the world that wasn't where I was; provided a kind of filter. Once or twice I might have made more of an effort, I suppose - and especially with Renee. But that would have been a real game changer, and that wasn't what I wanted. And remember, I'd found the person I was really looking for some years previously...

"'Any regrets?' How long have you got? How long have I got?! Not really. A proverbial roller-coaster, some bits I'm more proud of than others. The last few years in Australia were good; most of the years before that, pretty crappy.

"'What about Edward?' What about Edward? I thought he was a tosser in ninety-six; I thought he was a tosser even before then. Chances are that he's still a tosser now. He may not be, of course. But you know what, I don't give a toss myself. Which, I suppose, makes me the tosser at the end of the day, doesn't it?

"Goodbye, brother dear."

Impartial Certainties

(December 2013)

"Who's it from?"

"Sorry?" He was staring at the small sheaf of folded paper he somehow still seemed to be holding in his hand and had not registered her arrival into the room.

"I saw it on the kitchen table," she said, the lightness in her voice in sharp contrast to how heavy the letter now felt. "It's not very often you get mail from overseas any more. Who do you know in Dubai?"

"Dubai?"

"That was the postmark. I noticed it." She had walked round behind his chair and took her own on the other side of the fireplace. As she sat down she pulled her cardigan close as if settling in for a story-telling session by the fire. "So, who do you know in Dubai?"

"Dubai? No-one. It wasn't sent from there," he said, somewhat absently, then corrected himself. "Of course it *was* sent from there, but it originated somewhere else."

"Where was that?"

He looked at the first page again to verify there was no clue.

"I don't know."

"How mysterious!" she said with a slight lilt in her voice. It was the tone to which she always defaulted when suppressing a giggle. She was - as she had told him on a number of occasions - now too old to giggle. "A letter from an unknown source and an unknown location. I like a good mystery. Are there any clues?"

"Clues? Somewhere between Africa and America - so Asia probably."

"That's not much to go on," she suggested.

"I suspect not Australia - if only because there's so much about Australia in the letter. I think Singapore, but that's only a guess."

"A guess? Based on?"

He looked up at her now, uncertain as to how far he should go, how deeply he should draw her in. He had, after all, been protecting her for so long now, keeping her away from what little emotional reside might remain. He had argued to himself that he had done so only to protect her, all the while knowing that his actions had been entirely selfish, an attempt to seal off the past, to bury it in concrete deep underground as if it were a time capsule intended for future discovery some millennia hence. If he told her who the letter was from - and how could he not? - he would still need to stop short of the whole truth. Her version of the truth differed somewhat from that of the letter's author, and only he had the full picture as it pertained to the three of them, a kind of puppeteer triangulating the past.

He felt a tug on his heartstrings.

"Based on who sent it."

"Who?"

She had lost the playful lilt because her urge to giggle had been driven away by the look in his eyes. After all these years - even though they had been good years by and large - she knew serious and she knew sadness, and it was a combination of the two she saw in him now.

"There's something wrong?"

It was statement bookended by question marks, as if it had been spoken in English yet written down in some archaic language its roots in Spanish.

"Yes, although it may have resolved itself by now." He looked at the first page. "The letter was dated four weeks ago."

"So," she tried again, a slight impatience creeping into her voice. He knew she hated it when he was obtuse. "Who's it from."

"Ralph," he said as flatly as he could manage, looking towards her to gauge the effect of his words. He delivered the whole punch. "It's from Ralph and he says he is dying. He may indeed," he paused for a final effect, "be dead by now."

"Ralph!" She had moved her hand to her mouth. "But I thought..."

"Yes," he said quickly, though he hoped not too quickly, "I'd assumed he was dead already. We knew he'd had those scrapes, and we hadn't heard anything…"

There was some meagre satisfaction in this being only a partial lie; he *was* aware of the rumours relating to some of his brother's more dubious business dealings - his 'scrapes' - however, Edward had been pretty certain that his brother was still alive even though they hadn't heard from him for years. Death, he knew, involved things like inquests and lawyers and wills, almost wherever you were. Had Ralph been already dead - dead before he had written the letter, as it were - then Edward felt confident he would have known about it. Even so, he had previously done nothing to disabuse Catherine of the notion that his brother had long since left this world, destination uncertain. If anything, he had encouraged that assumption.

If he were talking of evils, of course, then Edward's little subterfuge was the minor partner in his consortium of lies. Deliberately finding a way to feed Ralph the 'news' that Catherine had herself died had been his greatest gamble. Inevitably there had been calculation in it. Since Ralph's failure to show up at their wedding and his subsequent refusal to respond to any attempted contact, Edward was as certain as he could be that if either of them had drawn a line it had been his brother - and that he had done so with a determination not to cross it. As far as he was concerned, therefore, Ralph could go hang. From Edward's perspective the relationship had always been a little 'tilted' away from him, and Ralph writing himself out of the picture could only help simplify his life.

He had needed to be careful how he handled the situation back in 1993. It had only been two years since Ralph and Catherine were a couple, and Edward was well aware that she still held a soft spot for him even if the lustre of their initial coming together had worn off. He knew that Ralph's absence at the wedding was as black a mark as it were possible to make in Catherine's book, and had played on her subtly enough to ensure that she entered it there underlined and in permanent ink. Even so, she was essentially a caring and forgiving person, qualities which had been part of her attraction for him. As a generic skill, he found manipulation of people easy enough; it was, after all, part of his job. People were cogs in the vast machine he used to turn on a daily basis, the machine that served the business - and perhaps from time to time, that served him too. Edward was good at nudging and nurdling, and with Ralph offering no opposition, it was relatively straightforward to get all the emotional ducks lined up the way he wanted.

"What is it?" she asked, hand returned to her lap.

"What's what?"

"That he has. The illness that's killing him?"

"Or killed him," he suggested quietly, just to make the point. "He doesn't say. I assume it's cancer, but the letter is vague. Talks a bit about a hospital, his medication, and health insurance."

"Insurance?"

"Something that paid off. At least that's how he sees it. Typical Ralph."

There was a slight pause. Edward wanted her to leave him to contemplate the letter again, but she showed no signs of moving.

"What else does he say?"

"Oh, he talks about work a little. How he spent time in Australia after the fiasco with those investments we heard about." Edward thought about mentioning the book and Jack Watson, but doing so would open a door for Catherine to walk through. Worse than that, she could walk through it without him knowing.

"I think it's supposed to be some kind of farewell letter; almost an attempt to set the record straight. But..."
"But what?"

"I don't know. It reads as if he's saying his goodbyes to himself; as if he's laying out his achievements, totting them up, giving them a score. Maybe to see what he amounts to. He always did like the solidity of numbers. They meant something to him."

But now words too, Edward thought to himself, not losing sight of the book; that seemed like an achievement of some merit - not that he was going to openly acknowledge it. The title seemed an odd one; Edward wondered what he meant by using 'impartial' in it. "Overall I think he's angry, mainly. Not with his situation; he seems to accept that almost without question."

"With what then?"

"Angry with me." Edward thought about those evenly distributed references and barbs, as if his brother had to keep coming back to them to stay on track, to honour the purpose of his letter, making sure Edward knew how pissed he was with him, and that, even in his final hour, he was not forgiven.

"About what?"

He glanced towards the mantle clock to register the time, then smiled sadly at her.

"About you."

"Me?"

He nodded. He knew he didn't need to refer back; scars like that never go away. Just by referencing it, Catherine would feel the jab of pain again.

"But it wasn't your fault," she said.

"It wasn't anyone's fault," he offered in reply. He didn't wish her to feel any guilt. He never had.

There was another pause. This time she rose then turned and looked out of the window for a moment. Turning back, she walked towards the door.

"It was everyone's fault," she countered from somewhere behind him, then left the room preventing any response.

The peculiarity of his situation was, he realised, that he could 'do' nothing. As Edward started to skim through the letter again he was struck by the notion that, whatever Ralph had said in it, he was powerless to act. He couldn't write back or go and see him. All he could do was wait; wait for the final news that would come one day, relatively soon. It was like boxing with both hands tied behind your back: you couldn't defend yourself, you couldn't retaliate. Ralph had all the power in this, his final exchange. That felt a little strange to Edward, especially as he had grown up in the dominant position, always able to direct, instruct, cajole his younger sibling. He had over-stepped the mark more than once - what older brother doesn't? - but it had not been a particularly unusual relationship, not from what he could see.

Taken in that context, the letter represented at best a final, if pyrrhic victory for Ralph. Too much water had flowed under their individual bridges for it to make very much difference to Edward. So what that his brother had sworn at him, refused to forgive him, taunted him for being just out of reach? He was seventy-one years old now; too old to care. Too close to his own denouement to be concerned whether his brother was dying in Cambodia or Katmandu. Perhaps, from that perspective, the letter had singularly failed; perhaps it had succeeded in achieving the exact opposite of that which had been intended. If Ralph's aim had been to make Edward feel somehow guilty or regretful or filled with remorse, all it had achieved was to allow Edward the luxury of reaffirming that it made not a jot of difference to him. Even if Ralph had been pleading for a death bed reconciliation and divulged exactly where he was holed-up, Edward was pretty certain he would simply have stayed put and - to borrow Ralph's terminology - 'let the fucker die'.

What he did not know, of course, was the effect it would have on Catherine - not that he had any intention of letting her read it. Might she, in defence of her husband, be returning to that little black book of hers and re-emphasise the indelible mark already made there? Or might she - out misplaced remorse, contrition, guilt - be trying to expunge the entry, its removal an admission to something unnameable on her side? Edward could not know. Worse than that, he would be unable to find out; it wasn't, after all, the kind of question you could ask outright - even if you happened to know how to frame it. He would look for signs; that was all he could do.

Did Ralph 'count' in the end? That had been one of his questions. On one level - the familial, the factual - of course he counted, Edward could never deny that. But on the level to which Ralph was referring? Did he 'count' to Edward as a 'special' person and was he doing so at that precise moment in time? He thought not. But maybe Ralph was asking himself that question; did he 'count' to himself? That would explain all the talk about Australia, the book, 'finding himself'. Edward could imagine, even after all this time, self-recognition as being someone who ultimately 'counted' would be of value to his brother.

There were no loose ends as far as Edward could see. He had been vaguely amused that Ralph had once tried to 'be like him' - whatever that meant. Ralph didn't really have any idea about how Edward had been at work, in 1993 or at any time since then. And rather than flattered by the suggestion, it seemed merely another example as to how Ralph's reality differed from his own. Perhaps it had always been thus. Perhaps as unexciting as he was, Edward still held the upper hand in spite of everything. Perhaps that's what the last two decades of Ralph's life had actually been all about: catching up his older brother, besting him, showing off, demonstrating that they were, after all, equals.

Smiling, Edward folded the pages and retuned them to their envelope. Equals they never would be, he still had Catherine after all.

The Dam Buster

(August 1952)

"Don't do that."

The boy looked up. Momentarily blinded by the sun, he lifted a damp sandy hand to his forehead to combat the glare. The girl was walking purposefully towards him. He had seen her there yesterday too, recognised her green swim suit. She was still a few yards away, so he ignored her and bent to his task once more.

"I said, don't do that. You mustn't."

"Why not?" he asked, pulling another large stone from the pile he had collected and finding it a suitable home in the dam he was constructing.

"Just don't," she said.

He saw the blue of her plastic sandals arrive in his peripheral vision and stop just a couple of feet from him, the other side of a ribbon of water that was running across the sand towards the sea.

"Don't," he said.

"Don't what?"

"Don't kick my dam. Please."

The last word seemed to still the foot he felt certain was just about to fly into the wall he was building.

"Why not?" she asked. "What are you doing anyway?"

She crouched down, the light reflecting off her costume seeming to shade everything a lurid green.

"Building a dam," he said, selecting another stone, studying it and then examining the wall to see where it might best fit.

"Why?"

"To stop the water, of course."

She watched him ease the next stone into place, padding sand around it as if it were cement. It looked like a good wall.

"Why?"

He looked up. She was not looking at him now, intent on the water, watching it flow towards the wall then ripple and eddy as it found a way around.

"To stop it," he repeated. "Then I'm going to dig out a big hole here" - he indicated a loose circle already marked out with a few shells - "and make a lake. Then I'll have lots of water."

"What do you want water for?" Her tone was dismissive. It irritated him. "And the sea's only just there, stupid."

The word irked him.

"Because the tide's going out. And when it's gone out it will be a long way away. And I want sand here for my sandcastles. See?"

Nearby there were two buckets - one with a crenelated base - and two shovels. The buckets were clean and dry. She could tell that they were new; her buckets didn't look like that.

"Okay. I see," she said.

She stood up and edged out of his sight. He looked up, not trusting her; expecting her to suddenly come running and jump into his dam. She had moved closer to the shallow cliff wall and the source for the stream. Absentmindedly, she pulled at a couple of stones from near where the water emerged. A small clutch of pebbles dropped to the shingle beneath.

From their separate vantage points they watched the water now weave a little differently, though it still hit the wall where he was building.

"It won't work," she said, definitively.

"Why not?"

He had placed his last free stone and was walking towards the base of the cliff to find some fresh ones. She picked one up from near her feet and handed it to him. He took it without a word. It was a good one, large, and with a nice shape; some jagged edges that would make it easy to bed into the sand.

"It just won't," she said, not prepared to elaborate.

He picked up two more large stones and headed back to his wall.

"What's your name?" she asked, looking after him.

"Why?"

"Isn't it nice to know people's names?" She paused. "My name's Penny. Penny Wilson. Actually it's Penelope, but no-one calls me that because I hate it." She paused again. "What's yours?"

Her large stone fitted brilliantly at the edge of the wall. He cemented it in and watched the ripple and flow of the water change a little. He was grateful.

"Edward," he said.

"Oh," she sounded disappointed. "What do your friends call you?"

"What?"

"What do your friends call you?" She said a little louder, then picked up another stone and headed back towards him.

He glanced up. It was a really big one. If she wanted, she could have just dropped it right there and destroyed everything.

"Edward," he said, his voice flat and even, holding out his hands for the stone she held.

She passed it to him.

"Thank you," he said. He knew it was good to be polite, even to girls in bright green swimming costumes who scared you a little bit.

"Can I help?"

He placed it down in the sand next to him. It was a beauty; perfect to serve as the anchor the far end of the wall. That was two great stones she had brought him.

"Sure," he said, trying to be a little more upbeat. "You want to dig?"

"Dig!" She sounded excited suddenly, as if he had entrusted her with a big responsibility.

"Where the shells are. That's the edge of the lake. If you start digging the hole just at the end there, and I'll start letting a little water through."

"And then come towards the wall?"

"Here." He stood up and drew a marker on both sides of the little stream about a foot from the dam wall. "If you dig all the way to there and I'll finish the wall."

"And then we'll dig the rest out together?"

Edward made a sound that was supposed to indicate he was agreeing with her, but it was far from convincing. The subtlety was beyond Penny however, and she had already made for his bucket and spades.

"Can I use these?" she asked.

He nodded.

"But not the red one. The red one's mine."

For the next few minutes they worked in tandem. Having removed one small stone from the base at the centre of the wall to allow it to flow a little, Edward was now on a relay to the base of the small cliff to collect stones which he then used to strengthen his dam. Penny was digging out spadefuls of increasingly wet sand from the growing reservoir and setting these neatly aside in a pile beside her.

"We might be able to use this sand for building later," she suggested.

Edward hadn't considered the building part yet; he hadn't said anything to her about building. But she was digging quickly and well, and the pool of water was expanding just as he had imagined it would.

"You're a good digger," he said.

"You're a good builder."

As the reservoir grew, so the pattern on the surface of the water changed. When the stream hit the sudden depth of the growing pool, rivulets that had once existed just disappeared, replaced by invisible eddies beneath the surface. At the face of the wall, frustrated by the small hole he had made for it so far, the breadth of water Edward had to keep back was gradually growing as it strove to find a way around the edges of the dam. He was still losing some, but he thought these were now smaller trickles. Maybe Penny had been right about it not working, but he felt he was losing much less than before, and the lake she was digging out was still growing.

He lifted the really big stone and stepped round to the far side, placing it down in the sand where he wanted the wall to end. That would be his limit. There was a gap of about a foot he still needed to fill. He stood up, ready to run back to the cliff to get some more large stones. Having reached his markers, Penny had stopped digging and had stood up too.

"More stones?" she asked. He nodded and they ran together to the base of the cliff.

"We need really good ones," Edward said, resisting the temptation to pick up the first ones he saw. The girl had found some fine stones already and he wondered if this might be her special talent. He believed everyone had a special talent; that's what his father had told him.

"Where are you from, Edward?"

"Winchester," he said definitively, the way he always did when he was certain of something.

"Where's that?"

"It's where King Arthur's Round Table is."

"King Arthur," she repeated. "That's Lancelot too, isn't it? And the sword in the stone?" She saw him nod. "Thought so. That's a long way from here."

"Hours."

"Isn't there a castle near here too? King Arthur's castle?"

"Camelot." His father had told him the story and said that Arthur's castle was near where they were going on holiday. They hadn't seen it yet, but Edward hoped they would, even if it was a ruin. But the car had been playing up and needed fixing again, which was why they had walked down to the beach three days in a row even if doing so was problematic with baby Ralph.

"I wish I was Arthur's Queen," she said, her voice suddenly sparkling.

Edward looked at her. She was about the same height as him, even though he knew she was a little older. In her arms she was cradling three very large stones. With the ones he had collected, that would be enough.

"She was called Guinevere," he said. "She was very beautiful." He wasn't sure why he added that last part, so suddenly said "Come on; let's finish the wall!" and ran away from her.

They piled their stones a safe distance from the edge of the wall and Edward set about bridging the remaining gap. Penny passed him the stones one at a time, fascinated to see the methodical way in which he worked. Soon the wall was complete; Edward then plunged his hands into the base of the pool now created in front of it and dragged handfuls of wet sand upwards to layer against the stone edifice as if it were some kind of render. Then he stood up and took a step back.

The wall was almost four feet wide and in places stood nearly six inches proud of the water's surface. At either end, the escaping liquid had already worn out two shallow channels that weaved away from them, petering out some twelve feet further on as it was sucked into the drying sand. Immediately behind the centre of the wall the sand was darker where the water was running toward Penny's lake. He knew he had succeeded in stopping the stream as well as he could. The reservoir seemed a little shallower than before, but it still looked good.

"Let's finish the lake," he said making a sudden dash for his red spade.

For a few minutes they both dug, deepening the reservoir and increasing the pile of damp sand away to the side. It was brief frenetic activity accompanied by laughter. At some imperceptible signal they stopped. Edward dropped his spade and then lay face down in the sand, getting his eye-line as close to the rim of the water as he could. It gave him a different perspective; it made him feel small, and the dam wall much larger.

"Shall we make sandcastles now?" Penny asked from over his shoulder.

"You can start," he said, suddenly comfortable and absorbed.

"Can I use your buckets?"

"Yes."

Edward focused on the surface of the water, watching the little ripples, evidence of current and direction of flow, trying to imagine what was going on within the water itself. He could see that the level of the pool was very gradually - almost imperceptibly - falling, and he tried to focus on the far edge of his lake to visually capture the receding water almost grain by grain. He knew he would need to release a little more water through the wall. Behind him came the sounds of shovelling followed by the tell-tale thump as the upturned bucket hit the sand, then the tapping of the spade on the its base.

He didn't really like the seaside. He hated the sea, but the ice creams were good. He didn't like crowds either, and soon became bored, uncomfortable. Building the dam had saved him today. Although he hadn't told Penny, doing so had been his father's idea. "Something to keep you busy" he had said. He knew it would appeal to him.

Kneeling back up, he turned. Penny had already built four individual sandcastles and was filling the bucket for a fifth. They were disconnected from each other and the angles between them were offset, which annoyed him. He would have sited them parallel to each other. It didn't look like any kind of fortification he had ever seen or imagined, more like a village.

He had an idea.

"Why don't we make a road between them? That might look good."

Penny shook her head, not sure what he meant.

Edward picked up the spare spade and with the back of it began to flatten out the sand between her castles, taking care not to damage them. Once he had made roads between the first three she could see what he meant.

"That looks really good!" she said, approvingly. "We could make a whole city!"

"And have a road leading to the lake," he suggested. "That's where the people could get their water for drinking and cooking."

Penny set to making more sandcastles with renewed vigour, taking the trouble to embellish them so that they looked like houses. As she built, Edward followed on, adding to the road network. From the little stream where he had started, their empire now spread out to encompass an impressive area. The sea was now a long way away, and most people had moved their things further down the beach to be closer to the water. Where they were was now relatively quiet.

"That's impressive," said a voice. They both looked up.

"Hello," said Penny.

"Hello." It was Edward's father. Edward had paused briefly, recognising the voice, but had almost immediately returned to his civic duties. "Who are you?"

"My name's Penny," said the girl. "Who are you?"

"I'm Edward's father," he said, making a show of looking around of their efforts. "That's pretty impressive. Great dam building, Edward."

His son said nothing, concentrating on completing the last few inches of road to the reservoir. When he had done so, he stood up, spade in hand.

"We have to go," the man said, "Mummy needs to get Ralph back to the cottage." Edward didn't move.

"Oh," said the girl. She looked at Edward. "Will you be back tomorrow?"

"Don't know," he replied.

She waited a moment.

"Can I carry on building, Edward? If I get my own bucket and spade?"

Edward's father had begun to move away, so the boy was obliged to follow after him.

"Yes, if you like."

She immediately ran off across the sand to the windbreak behind which her own parents were sitting on their deckchairs reading. She paused to take a drink, then collected her bucket and spade and ran back towards their construction site.

She stopped a few feet short. The dam wall had been breached and three of her castles had been broken.

Edward was nowhere to be seen.

Duty Free

(July 2009)

Once upon a time she had liked airports. She had been thinking that a great deal recently that there seemed to be a kaleidoscope of things she had enjoyed 'once'. But airports would have been back in the days when she was travelling herself, when her experience involved walking beyond the big sign that said 'Departure Gates' and which, obtusely, was more about the promise of an arrival somewhere else. The sign said 'Passengers Only' in smaller letters; she wasn't sure that had always been the case, but you can't trust memory can you? Not travelling herself, she had to be satisfied with tootling around the shops on this side of security. She wasn't sure 'tootling' was her style either, but it seemed expected of her these days, and if it helped them out by keeping Georgia occupied for a little while, well that was all right. Even though Georgia was less than a third her age - and at twenty-one should have been perfectly capable of managing herself - Penelope had been given the task (via one of those whispered, side-of-the-mouth requests) to take her grand-daughter off for a few minutes while they sorted out a minor issue with the number of their bags, or their weight, or something.

It was a task she immediately felt beyond her. For one thing Georgia didn't seem to *need* anything, and for another the selection of retail outlets here on 'the dull side' of the airport left Penelope underwhelmed. She could tell Georgia wasn't keen, but she had gone along with the proposal largely because it was, from her perspective, the lesser of two evils. It wasn't that she didn't love her Gran, she did - but at that moment she simply loved the idea of walking under the 'Departure Gates' sign a little more.

They nosed in W.H.Smith's - which had been very busy and made Penelope a little flustered - and then through Claire's. It was probably in there that Georgia had the idea about the bangle, having been in-part bribed to undertake the current exercise by the potential of a 'going away present'. The present had been her grand-mother's idea; her father had just asked her to look after his mother as he was concerned she was looking a little 'peaky'.

It was in Accessorize that Penelope's peakiness became a wobble, and having knocked over a small stand of purses as she reached out for support, Georgia found herself leading her gran, arms linked, to some nearby seats.

"Thank you, Dear," Penelope said, endeavouring to rein in her breathing. "Wasn't it warm in there! Do you think you could get me some water?"

"It's OK, Gran," Georgia said as the elder woman began to fumble with her bag. "Back in a tick."

As she headed back to Smith's, Georgia looked down the departure hall to see if her parents were anywhere handy, but failed to locate them through the mass of randomly moving heads.

Two minutes later she returned.

"Sorry it's warm," she said, handing the bottle over. "All the cold ones were gone."

"Don't worry, that's fine Dear, thank you."

Georgia removed the cap after Penelope had briefly struggled with it and then watched her grandmother take a sip. It was odd how older people drank straight from a bottle, demurely, as if it were the height of bad manners to do so.

"Did you see anything you liked?" Penelope asked.

"There was one in Claire's that I wouldn't mind taking another look at - but in a minute's fine." She had added the last phrase as Penelope had given every indication of rising immediately to re-enter the fray.

Penelope took another sip of water then replaced the cap on the bottle.

"I had a boy give me a bangle at an airport once," she said in a matter-of-fact manner.

"Was that Granddad?"

"Oh no, Dear, of course not!" Penelope laughed.

"Gran!"

"What's wrong, Dear? I used to be young once too you know. And is it so bad to have a boy buy you something?"

"No, of course not."

"Well then. I bet you'd let that Daniel buy you something, wouldn't you?"

"Danny?" She seemed struck by the impossibility of the idea. "I don't think that's quite Danny's style, Gran."

She didn't mention that she and Danny were going through something of a difficult patch, a large part of her doubting she would ever see him again. She picked up the thread.

"So if it wasn't Granddad, who was it? I'm intrigued."

Penelope laughed softly.

"Oh there was no intrigue about it, I can assure you of that. He was just a nice young man I met once when I'd been away on my holidays. I say young man, but he was just a little bit older than me. I would have been about your age."

"So before Granddad then?"

"Before Rupert? Possibly. Well certainly before he and I were 'an item', I think the phrase is. I had gone on holiday to Paris with my sister. It had been just a little risqué of us going off together, of course. My parents weren't at all happy about it, to tell you the truth. But we were old enough. It was the Sixties after all, and just about everything was changing. A year after Paris the Beatles had their first number one record I think. Must seem like ancient history to you."

Penelope put her hand on her granddaughter's arm. Georgia knew this was one of her little signals; she could stop right there and they would move on, or she could tell a little more of the story.

"Was he French then?"

"No. Funnily enough he was American. Peggy and I met him as we were going around some gallery or other. He bumped into Peggy, nearly sent her flying. He was very gallant and had such a wonderful accent. Peggy made a play for him straight away, of course. In those days anything in a pair of trousers was fair game for Peggy. She never learned her lesson."

"But he was interested in you?"

"He bought us a coffee, to make up for his clumsiness he said. It was all very romantic, sitting by the Seine, our first time outside of England, drinking with a strange American." Penelope smiled. She was caught in one of those 'once' moments, but was happy to play it out for Georgia. "He asked if he could see us the next day and of course we said yes. The three of us went to the Louvre together; he seemed to know a great deal about art and history. Peggy was smitten, but she could see that he liked me better."

A sudden blast from the airport tannoy prompting passengers for Dubai to proceed through Departures threatened to drag Georgia and Penelope from their bubble. Georgia resisted.

"What was his name?"

"Brad. Isn't that so American?" Penelope laughed. "He lived in Wisconsin - which meant nothing to us of course - and he told us that he'd been touring Europe for a few weeks. Paris was his last stop before he went back home to take up the reins on his family farm. It sounded as if it was as big as Hampshire!"

"And the bangle?"

"Oh yes. Well, it so happened that he was due to fly back home the same day as us, so we went to the airport together. At one point Peggy excused herself to go the Ladies, and Brad suddenly presented me with this little box. Said he had been carrying it around for days. I must have gone bright red!"

"Was it nice, the bracelet?"

"Beautiful. Plain, quite simple, but very elegant. He had bought it when we were in the Louvre but neither of us had noticed. It was a pale golden colour with some little red stones inset. There was a note inside the box. I didn't read it until I got home and was alone in my bedroom. I didn't want to let Peggy see, of course."

"What did the note say? Was it a love letter, Gran?"

"Love letter indeed," Penelope laughed. "It was just his address and a little message..."

"Which said?"

"Which said: 'Dearest Penny, I hope you will come and see me at home on the farm'. That was all."

Georgia squeezed her grandmother's hand.

"But that's so romantic!"

"Wasn't it sweet of him?"

"And did you? Go to America, I mean?"

Unscrewing the cap on her bottle, Penelope took another sip then smiled ruefully as she replaced it.

"No, Dear, I didn't. I've never been to America. We got home and then, well, then your grandfather sort of happened, and that was that."

"That's so sad," Georgia said.

"Is it, Dear? I'm not so sure. I've been very lucky really. Rupert was a wonderful man, and we had your father and your uncle Charlie - and that means we've got you." She squeezed Georgia's hand. "Would I change any of that?" She paused. "I don't think so."

From somewhere nearby there was a shout in a voice Georgia recognised. She looked round and saw her father heading their way. As she was about to stand up, Penelope's hand stopped her for a moment.

"But take my advice, Dear. If ever anyone buys you a bracelet with a note inside it asking you to go to Wisconsin, then go."

"Did you buy anything?" Georgia's father said as he reached them.

"Only water," said Penelope as she put out her hand for him to help her up, then turning to Georgia said "But we had a nice chat about airports, didn't we, Dear?"

"And bracelets."

Superheroes

(March 2011)

The sound from the city entered the room through the open balcony windows accompanied by the quiet conversation of Françoise and Gerd who, having gone outside to smoke, were sitting on small wrought iron chairs and, in the absence of a table - the balcony being far too small - balancing their cigarette packets on their knees. The music sounded less exuberant now. Several hours had passed since the musicians had started their torch-lit parade through the city. The lightening of the sky seemed to accompany a reduction in verve.

She had been generally amazed; first at the spectacle, and second that she was there to witness it. Being in Basel had never been part of their itinerary; that she was there for Fasnacht was simply luck. When Claire had decided to stay in Zurich rather than continue on to Amsterdam for their final stop as planned, Georgia and Alice had been faced with a decision: honour Amsterdam or go straight home. Georgia, who had become exhausted with the sheer intensity of their trip, had favoured the latter, but Alice had been inclined towards the Dutch capital. It was, she argued, an adventure; better not to end it with a whimper. In the end they agreed to travel home by train - and to go via Basel. It was a compromise of sorts. Alice had argued that they had seen surprisingly little of trains and nothing of Switzerland, and Georgia knew that an unplanned diversion along the way appealed to her sense of the unrehearsed.

She had no idea where Alice was now. Presumably in a crowd somewhere, or in a bar, or having one last 'fling' as she liked to describe her more casual acquaintances.

"You are here for Fasnacht?" the woman at the slightly shabby hotel had asked as she handed over the keys to the last available twin room and explained how to get into town using the trams.

"Fas-what?" Alice had replied.

It was only later, as they sat in a bar near the Barfüsserplatz that Christoph and Maxime had explained the Basel carnival to them. By then - it had been just after 3 a.m. - the city was filling up considerably. The bars were packed. They had met the two men when sharing a table in a hotel bar near the station around midnight. Soon, Maxime had said, all the city lights would be switched off and people would start marching; drummers and piccolo players with crowds of people, many in costumes, carrying elaborately decorated lanterns.

"It used to be a religious festival," he explained, already having to shout loudly to be heard, "hundreds of years ago. But now we just celebrate it as a carnival. It's Basel's party time."

Georgia had been unable to establish why it started in the middle of the night, and the fact that it carried on for a number of days was daunting. They were only going to be there for one night - which meant they would probably spend much of the journey back to Paris and then London asleep! At least their train out of Basel was a late one.

Alice had gone off with Maxime at some point a little after they had left the bar to watch the parade. "There are thousands here. People always are getting separated," Christoph had warned, and had insisted that she and Alice had both the address of their hotel and his own address and phone number. Later he had said to Georgia "Maxime is a good man. Your friend is safe."

She had liked Christoph instantly. Although older than her by a few years (she guessed ten or so) he had the kind of face and physique that would probably look the same at forty as it had at twenty. He was quiet, not in a shy or fearful way, but rather from self-confidence, as if he had nothing to prove to himself nor anyone else. There was no need for flamboyance or exaggerated showiness. He dressed well, casually, and was well-groomed - all in a relaxed fashion. He had splendid hands with immaculate fingernails. Even though she was still only twenty-three, Georgia had come to believe you could tell a lot about a man from his hands.

He had taken hers briefly as they had darted across a road between two groups of marching revellers. It was a hand that felt solid and confident, and gave her a sense of safety and security. She would have happily continued to hold it once they had crossed the road, but he had let hers drop. She felt surprisingly disappointed.

They had watched the players for a little while, a one point eating waffles and crepes from a street stall. Georgia's phone had vibrated in her pocket. It was a message from Alice. "Am fine. C u back at hotel abt 8." She had leant towards Christoph to show him, and he had smiled as if to say "See?".

"Coffee at my place?" he had proposed to Françoise and Gerd who they had collected along the way, and, by smiling at her, she assumed she was also invited. She had tried to take his hand again. "It's complicated," he had said as he squeezed it and then let it fall again, his smile both a little apologetic and a little rueful.

She had wondered what 'complicated' meant though she didn't doubt it was the mot juste. His English was exceptional, which seemed to be the norm with all the people she had met there. Françoise, who was French and from just over the border in Colmar had perhaps the weakest English, but made up for it with her fantastic accent. Gerd's was strong and precise, infused with the occasional Germanic word order. Both he and Christoph were from Basel, though you wouldn't have known that listening to them; Christoph's accent seemed to defy location.

"I spent a year in London," he said as they sat down to drink coffee, Gerd making his way to the balcony to join Françoise who was leaning out over its railing to see if she could see any of the procession. "It was part of my education."

"But you've been back since?" Georgia asked, fairly certain his fluency could not only have been gained through a single visit to the UK and by being resident in Basel, multi-cultural though it was.

"Oh yes," he laughed, lightly, "many times. I even lived in the north for a couple of years. I hope to go back."

"What do you do?"

"I am very lucky," he said, waiving his arm around to indicate his sitting room, inviting her to take it all in and draw her own conclusions.

She had simply followed them in through the front door and up the steps. Her focus had been on making sure she was welcome and not in the way; she didn't want to appear the naive, gauche English tourist. Bidden to do so, she looked at the room. It was actually very large and with tall ceilings; the furniture was relatively sparse but clearly of good quality. There were some vases and small sculptures discretely placed among the books on the bookcase which dominated one wall. She wondered how she had missed that. And on the walls, paintings not prints. Involuntarily she felt the fabric of the chair in which she sat; leather, good leather. Money.

He laughed at her.

"My father is a successful businessman. Books, paintings, antiques, things like that are a bit of a hobby for him. I sort of 'help out' from time to time.'

"Help out?"

"I have a good eye, I suppose. I'm well-educated, well-read. I can usually see a bargain - or spot something that's pretending to be what it isn't. And I have a hunch which is right more often than not."

"I see," she said, not really seeing at all.

"My education, for example. Fine Arts at University in Lausanne. I had a year in London. My time in the north of England? Working out of one of our subsidiary offices. Mainly it was about taking the family name into meetings; sometimes finding things. People." He sipped at his coffee, confident that she wasn't quite there yet. "Take Gerd."

"Gerd?"

"Yes." Simultaneously they looked towards the figures on the balcony. Gerd was stroking Françoise's hair; they were silent. "Gerd is quite an artist. Sorry," he corrected himself, "Gerd *could be* quite an artist. One day. He has talent. My father is sponsoring him for a little while, to give him some space to see if he can 'find' himself."

Georgia remained fixed for a moment on the image Gerd and Françoise were creating. When she turned back, Christoph was looking at her.

"The picture against the far wall? One of Gerd's. You should take a look at it before you leave."

It was an innocuous statement, delivered innocently, but its clarity was not lost on her.

"You said 'a little while'. What does that mean?"

"Gerd?"

She nodded.

"He has probably until the end of the summer. These next three of four months are very crucial. I hope Françoise gives him space too. We want to be able to exhibit him before the end of September, but right now we don't have enough material - good quality material - to do so. But Gerd knows this."

"And if he doesn't deliver what you need?"

"C'est la vie."

He had delivered his answer in the same relaxed, easy-going, confident manner as he seemed to possess for everything else, yet it struck Georgia how cold and calculating the sentiment was beneath it.

"Isn't that a little brutal?" She had struggled for the word and settled on 'brutal' even though that wasn't entirely what she meant.

"Not at all," Christoph's smile was completely devoid of any malice. "Gerd knows the agreement; it's perfectly fine. There is no threat or animosity. I like Gerd, very much. I'm sure I will continue to see him after September whatever happens."

"'Whatever happens'," she echoed.

"But this is business. It is nothing personal. Nora Ephron."

Georgia was stumped.

"Nora?"

"Nora Ephron. Great American writer and director. 'You've Got Mail'. Tom Hanks and…"

"Meg Ryan," she interjected, keen to show she could be on his wavelength. "Yes. And 'When Harry met Sally'..."

"And 'Sleepless in Seattle'. Precisely. You remember the part in 'Mail' where Hanks tells Ryan to fight, not realising he is telling her to fight *him*? 'It's business, not personal'; that's what he says, something like that."

"And that makes it okay?"

Christoph leant forward in his chair, concern on his face.

"Makes what okay?"

"To treat Gerd as if he were - I don't know..."

"You ask him," he suggested. "When he comes back in from whispering love to Françoise, you ask him. See if he thinks he is being taken advantage of, or whether he thinks this is the chance of a lifetime."

It was immediately apparent to her that she wouldn't need to; that Gerd would be effusive and grateful for the support he was getting. Christoph was probably his knight in shining armour. There was still something nagging at her, however. She knew that she was about as far away from a business person as it was possible to get and therefore her perspective was more idealistic than anything else, but even if Gerd was grateful, there was something that didn't ring true for her.

"I don't think I'll have to ask him," she suggested. Christoph shrugged his shoulders a little, smiled, and eased himself back into his chair. "I'm sure he's very grateful, and that he'll produce lots of good things for you to sell."

"But?"

"'But'?"

"I sense you have a 'but' lurking, Georgia. That even though Gerd is happy with the arrangement and I am happy with it, that you have a reservation. Am I right?"

Georgia looked back out onto the balcony. They were smoking again, their conversation resumed.

"Look, I don't know anything about art, or sculpture, or business..."

"More than you suspect," he interrupted, "I guarantee that!"

"Perhaps. But I'm not sure they mix. I suppose I grew up believing in things like writing and painting in a different way to everything else. That they were special because people had talents the rest of us lacked. There was never any cross-over into things that might be construed as 'commercial'."

"Ah, the Artist as God!" He said it smilingly, but with something of a tone that she could not help but notice. "More coffee, by the way?" She shook her head. "Yes, of course. And if I'm honest, me too. The notions we have of these fantastic people. Rubens, Van Gogh, Gaugin, Picasso! Well maybe not Picasso! Romantic, yes? We placed them up onto these pedestals didn't we, as if they were gods. We only thought of them as painters, not people; painters who made wonderful images. And writers too. Shakespeare, Hardy, Eliot, Ibsen, Maupassant. They were somehow super-heroes. Yes, I think that is the word: Superheroes! We were never taught to consider them as just people who lived lives the same as we do; had to endure the same boring things, the same drudgery. But they did. Of course they did! Some of them - the lucky ones - may have had patrons who protected them from such trivia. Isn't that all my father and I are doing here, with Gerd and others?"

Even though she sensed he might be correct in what he was saying and that the parallel he was drawing was probably a perfectly reasonable one, there was still disquiet in her. Not aimed perhaps at Christoph, but at something much larger and wider.

"But you make it sound so cold. So commercial."

"Because it is. Because it always has been. Gerd doesn't have to worry about earning money for the moment because we support him. We give him the time to be a Superhero. There is a transactional nature about the arrangement, of course. Is that unfortunate? If you were idealistic, yes. But practically? I think it works perfectly. And there is absolute clarity on both sides."

She wanted to respond but was unsure how to. Before she could speak, Christoph called out to Gerd.

"Hey Gerd! Our pretty English friend here thinks that we shouldn't be supporting you. Thinks that we're some kind of modern-day slavers. Do you want not to have our money?"

"Are you a crazy man?" Gerd said, turning slightly on his chair. "How could I pay for my rent and my cigarettes if you were not there?" His laughter burst into the room and then was shared with the street as he turned back to Françoise.

"I'm sorry for that - but you see my point." Christoph placed his coffee cup down on the little table that sat between them. He leant forward again, placing a hand on her right arm. "I would love for the world to be as you might wish it to be. I really would. But it isn't, and it never has been. And you know, the thing that makes me okay with what we do - and how we try to do it - is that *we can*. As I said, I am lucky. Without that luck, without me meeting Gerd and people like him, without our help and assistance - however you might choose to view it - then where would Gerd be? How much smaller would his chances be of being what he *could* be?"

She nodded slowly and smiled. It was suddenly wonderful to feel his hand on her arm, and she wanted to know why it was 'complicated'; she wanted to feel as if she belonged in Basel; wanted Christoph to show her everything Fasnacht and the carnival had to offer. It was not the wealth, or his charm, or taste, or anything material; it was because she suddenly believed in him.

He moved his arm and the moment was gone.

"And now, my beautiful young English tourist, it is getting late - or it is getting early - and we need to get you back to your hotel. Alice will be worried about you." He stood up. "Let me see if I can find you a friendly taxi to get you safely where you need to be."

Bitter Coffee

(December 2016)

"Look, I'm going away for a few days after Christmas so I won't be around."

They were studying the dessert menus, trying to decide if they wanted another course or not. It was almost ritualistic, both of them knowing they'd had enough to eat and would settle for just coffee to round off the meal. It seemed as good a time as any to broach the subject.

"Oh? Where are you going?"

"I've found a little place up in the dales, on the edge of Cumbria. I'm sure it will be cold and damp and the weather will be awful."

"So why are you going if it will be so miserable?"

"I don't know," he said with the tone of a man who knew perfectly well why he was going.

"I'm sure you do, David," the younger man said with a slight wave of the menu he held in his left hand. "I don't think I've ever met anyone who knows as much about themselves as you do."

David laughed, just a little.

"Occupational hazard," he suggested.

A waiter, having misconstrued Christoph's gesture with the menu as a summons, appeared, notebook at the ready. Christoph looked to David, inviting the first commitment.

"Just coffee for me please - even though I know the desserts are brilliant."

"The same for me."

They had eaten there often enough over the past two years or so to know the menu inside and out, and to be able to speak to the quality of almost everything on it - and the desserts were consistently superb. Had he tried to think about when they had given up eating them, David may well have struggled to be definitive. Christoph would have been the better person to ask however; all their meals were expensed and Christoph had the records.

"So?" Christoph prompted.

David wasn't really in the mood for the interrogation he knew was inevitable; inevitable from the moment he decided on the trip to Hawes and, thus, the need to break the news to Christoph.

"I'm sorry I've nothing for you, Chris," he said, changing tack. "The last thing I tried was complete rubbish. And there have been one or two other beginnings that I haven't dared show you they're so bad. I thought that as my mojo seemed to have gone away on holiday, I might as well try the same cure."

"I'm not sure I believe that, if I'm completely honest."

"Which part?"

"The part about your mojo."

David smiled as he lifted the remnants of his wine to his lips.

"That's because you don't want to believe it."

There was a sudden peel of laughter from a nearby table that diverted their attention for a moment. The interruption was good, David felt; disrupting a certain momentum that their conversation was in danger of building.

"Who knows," he suggested, "I may just find something I want to write about while I'm walking the desolate moors…!"

"You're not Charlotte Bronte."

"More's the pity, eh? Anyway, I think you should just go home. Go back to Basel for Christmas and enjoy yourself. I'll be in touch when I get back from Hawes. Let you know if anything magical has happened. You don't need to hang around here to hand-hold me."

As soon as he said it, David realised the inappropriateness of the phrase. Of course that was exactly why Christoph wanted to be there, to hand-hold him. He had made that plain on more than one occasion.

"If I'm honest, I'm also worried," David pushed on, jumping into unplanned territory in order to cover his hand-holding faut pas. "Have you even considered the possibility that my first book was just a fluke? That I might be a 'one-hit-wonder', and that you're actually wasting your time - not to mention your money - on hoping there's a follow-up coming?"

"I have never considered that at all," Christoph said in a somewhat flat and dismissive tone, "because the person who wrote 'An Impossible Dilemma' couldn't be a 'one-hit-wonder', as you call it. Because that person had so much to say. It was evident on every single page."

"You are - as ever - too kind, Chris. But I fear you may be mistaken. I'm not one of your bright young things fresh out of school or college or wherever; someone who needs a helping hand - some helping cash - to get them on their feet. Compared to them I'm just an old man." He wanted to make himself less appealing, but without going too far. "I know we've talked about this before, but I simply don't need your assistance in that way. And before you say anything, I know your help is now limited to incidentals; meals like this, funding for the odd research trip, materials, whatever. But even that…"

It was a sore point, David knew that. He also knew that, where he was concerned, Christoph had struggled to keep the commercial and emotional separated. Struggled and failed. He had seen him in action with others; friend and patron one day, the next… In many ways he would have preferred such a stark transaction. It would have been cleaner, antiseptic. But Christoph had invested too much in him emotionally, and David knew that both were probably bad bets; at least one of them would certainly fail to bring him any reward. The image of a gambling addict came to mind; someone who couldn't help themselves but to chase losers, throw good money after bad. There might be a story there if he worked on it.

The coffee arrived; one large, heavy silver pot, plus a pot of cream and a small plate of amaretti.

"Elegant, as ever," David observed. It was a comment that could equally have been directed towards Christoph as to the coffee.

"What will you do when you go away to this miserable place after Christmas?" Christoph asked, a jarring note in his voice.

"Apart from trying to write?" David poured some coffee into both cups leaving himself space for cream. "Walk. Remind myself what nature looks like in that part of the world. Reconnect with something, hopefully. Try and keep warm!"

Christoph shook his head and looked down at his coffee.

David had history with that part of the world; history before he met Chris and fallen in to the universe of book-writing which he found consistently alien. His history in the Dales was with Diane and he needed his Swiss friend not to forget that. It was a way-marker that should have told Christoph the emotional path he was trying to navigate was a dead-end, overgrown, going nowhere. Might it have been otherwise once upon a time? David didn't know. It was a question he didn't want to try and answer.

"We used to spend most of our holidays there," he carried on, hoping that the reference to 'we' would be sufficient. "Used to walk for miles and miles, often in atrocious weather." He laughed as if recalling a memory, but it was hollow and false and just for show. "I daresay I couldn't walk as far these days."

"You could come back to Basel," Christoph suggested, "where it will be properly winter, not this awful, damp and dark imposter you English so adore!" He didn't try to disguise his distaste for the prospect, suddenly glad that David had forced him to make up his mind to go home. In that moment Basel seemed transformed into a sanctuary; as much as he loved England, he found it depressing. He knew he only kept coming back to see David. "We could go walking in the mountains; proper walking. See things you have never seen before. Walk the Rhine perhaps, or go skiing in Interlaken."

David could tell that there was as much enthusiasm behind Christoph's offer as there had been in the shallow laugh he had used to accompany his comments about walking in the rain. It felt as if they had crossed some kind of threshold bizarrely coinciding with the arrival of the coffee. He picked up his cup and sipped. It was dark and bitter, even with the cream. The emptiness of Christoph's offer gave him a chance to press the wedge home just a little further. He could have said 'yes'; said he would go to Basel, and the younger man would suddenly be energised, enthusiastic, move into planning mode. Whilst that would have been an easy option - and in many ways an attractive prospect - it would also have been dishonest, and David had no desire to prolong any dishonesty.

"Why don't we do this," he started teasing out the words, trying to arrive back at the decision he had already made in such a way as to allow it to be a joint one, an agreement. "Why don't we catch up after I come back from my miserable, cold, depressing time in the Dales - once I have recovered from the pneumonia I will undoubtedly catch! - and see where I've got to. If I find that I have something that I think is good enough, that there is something I've started working on that could be worthy of you and your father's continued faith in me, then fine. I will instantly come out to Basel. If not, then I really think, Chris, that it doesn't make any sense in you wasting your time and money on me any more. I really don't. I know that this is all to my disadvantage, but it just feels fair - and I respect you too much to be unfair to you."

He partly meant this and partly something else, of course. There was an underlying subtext. David had delivered his statement knowing that Christoph would be able to read between his very broad lines; to know that he wanted him to accept that his own hopes and ambitions were unlikely to be fulfilled, and move on too.

"And because you are an old man who doesn't really need our help?"

The reference to earlier in the conversation stung David a little. He was surprised.

"Money, no. But if I do manage to start on something that may indeed be worthy as a follow up to 'Dilemma' then I can't think of anyone else whose help I would rather welcome."

David left it there, an olive branch. He wanted to ensure there was as much of a distinction between money and help as there was between the two men themselves. He had never denied himself the somewhat bizarre luxury of knowing that Christoph appreciated him both as a writer and a man. It was flattering, and as a man nearly in his fifties, flattery was hard enough to come by.

He watched as Christoph nodded slowly then raised his coffee and drained it in a single gulp. It was an unusual gesture for someone who tended to savour such things, but David took it as a signal that he had, for the want of a better term, 'a deal'. He smiled and rose.

"Just popping to the gents."

He wasn't sure that he needed to go, but felt the separation provided a timely bookend to their conversation. There was no need for it to drag on any longer than necessary, and the last thing he wanted was to give Christoph a way back in, the chance to muster counter arguments. David knew himself to be a weak man, and, had Christoph tried really hard, he might find himself capitulating - which could only mean that he would have to re-engineer the conversation at some point in the future.

When he returned to the table Christoph's chair was vacant. The waiter sidled over.

"Your friend has settled the bill, Sir. He said he'd had a call and needed to go but that he would speak to you after Christmas."

"Thank you," said David, not bothering to take his own seat, rather pulling his jacket from where it hung over the back of the chair, "that sounds about right."

The street light on the other side of the road flickered uncertainly and David shivered against the sudden cold. It seemed strangely quiet, even for a midweek. A taxi went by, 'For Hire' light extinguished but devoid of passengers. From somewhere he could hear the distorted beat of music sounding momentarily louder as someone opened a door to go in or come out.

He paused. His favourite pub was a few hundred yards to the right; a similar distance to the left, the entrance to the car park where he had left his car. He weighed up his options, but there was ever only going to be one outcome this evening. Turning up the collar of his jacket, he tried to sink within its fabric, shrugged imperceptibly, and turned left.

www.ingramcontent.com/pod-product-compliance
Lightning Source LLC
Chambersburg PA
CBHW030755200726
48288CB00004B/1192